# THE UNFORGETTABLE ALEXANDRA SHAW

A. LLOYD SPANTON

The Unforgettable Alexandra Shaw
Copyright © 2023 by 25TUD10 Press

This is a work of fiction. Names, characters, places, and incidents are the product of the author's imagination or are used fictitiously.

Edited by Feral Girl Books
Copy Edited by EJL Editing
Cover Design by Qamber Designs & Media

Paperback ISBN # 978-1-7386857-1-4
eBook ISBN # 978-1-7386857-0-7

*Content Warning: Light suicidal ideation, emotional manipulation of a teen, mental health/trauma, off-page accidental death of an animal (not pet), underage drinking/drugs, mature language*

**www.alloydspanton.ca**

First Edition, 2023


10 9 8 7 6 5 4 3 2

# ONE

**THE IDEA THAT I** have no control over who I am makes me want to puke.

No, it makes me want to punch her first, for making us sit through this insufferable speech. Then I'll puke.

The way she's standing at the front of our class with her perfectly coiffed hair. Uniform pressed just right. Skirt exactly one inch below her knees. It makes my skin itch. She's the walking poster child for Pine Cliff Academy. She's perfection personified. I gag.

"In conclusion, scientists believe that both nature and nurture affect a person's character. That nurture expounds on what nature endows. Who we are, our personalities and individual identities, not to mention our future, are an accumulation of other people's influences and genetics and not, as many would like to believe, our own choice. Thank you."

The classroom erupts into applause as the tiny know-it-all frame of Kimberly Marshall steps out from behind the podium. All our eyes are on her and she's basking in the attention, something she doesn't get much of outside the classroom. She's bursting with words and opinions she can't wait to share with anyone who will listen.

Usually no one does, but today we have no choice but to listen. Held captive at our desks until the bell rings as student after student wax poetically about some preordained topic. A topic that our English teacher, Ms. Walker, assigned, proving Kimberly's point that we don't have any choice in anything whatsoever.

When the applause dies down, Kimberly returns to her seat in front of me. Her perky ponytail swings in my face and my stomach drops. My palms are slick with sweat. Any minute now, Ms. Walker will call my name, expecting me to take my place behind that podium with my rebuttal. An argument that we do have some sense of control over our fates, our identities, our personalities.

I believe this, I have to believe this. But it's hard enough to prove on the best of days. Even more so in front of a class of reform school kids who all wear the same iron-crisp uniforms, have the same haircuts, and listen to the same terrible music.

"Alexandra? Care to share your response on the Nature vs Nurture debate?" Ms. Walker's voice sounds distant, as if she's speaking to me from another plane, because I've left my body on the floor in a puddle of social anxiety. Slipped right out of myself, my world tipping one way, then the other.

I stand on wobbly legs, rub my palms on my tights. I force one foot in front of the other as I drag myself to the front of the class.

Everything is muted, a sea of distorted faces, one blurring into the next. They are my peers, but I am still getting to know these faces. I'm still the new kid, thrown into the awkward hierarchy of a new school six months ago. They are my peers, but they aren't exactly my friends.

I take a deep breath to try to push my body's natural responses away and nurture a calmer and collected presence. My argument, after all, is that we are in control of our own fate. Something I'll have already failed to prove if I can't even control my anxiety enough to get the words to leave my mouth.

"I, uh... Hi," I stammer, sweat starting to pool under my arms. My face flushes from the eyes pointed in my direction. "I'm Alexandra, and today I will be speaking to you about, uh, how humans have the capacity to defy both nature and nurture to write their own future?" The words are out, but I've lingered on the last one, my voice raised, turning my stance into a question. Mom would say I sound like there's nothing but empty space between my ears. Which are as hot as a stove burner, and likely just as red.

I glance desperately at Ms. Walker for help. She oozes cool; a short black bob, thick framed glasses that match the matte of the nose ring she wears with rebellious pride. She can't be much older than us. She has to know that she's putting us through hell, making us stand up here and defend our existence in the hierarchy of high school. Especially in a high school that's more of a reform school, full of troubled students who will do anything to rebel against the structure forced upon them.

Because that's what it all boils down to, doesn't it? It's not nature vs nurture; it's survival of the fittest. Those at the top always reign, while the rest of the outcasts are left to flail in their wake. Somehow, I managed to find my way to the top. I don't belong there, but I'm desperate to cling to the safety of it. Otherwise, this experience would be even more excruciating.

I'm staring, my words stalled to a stop. Ms. Walker motions gently with her hands for me to keep going, a small thumbs up of encouragement. But I'm a deer in headlights, the fluorescent beams on the ceiling screaming at me, and I can't remember a single thing I'm supposed to say.

"We—as humans, I mean… have the capacity to make choices and those choices are what secure our future. We grow and adapt and change depending on our experiences. Everything we do is an active decision that makes up who we are as, uh, humans."

A couple of muffled laughs, a few whispers. I'm clearly killing it up here. I take another deep breath, remembering where I'm supposed to take this argument. But my train of thought is derailed by the boy in the front row.

Kyle Larson.

Kyle is one of the reject jocks who thinks he's still the captain of the football team, even though there is no football team here. The Academy prefers we put our efforts into "more realistic things" such as academics. He's built like a linebacker, too, which he uses to his intimidating advantage.

Kyle was one of the first people I met when I started here, and that meeting is not something I remember fondly. I stood at my locker that first morning, my back to the hallway traffic as I fumbled with my lock, when a body slammed into me. I went flat against the locker, dropping all my books, instinctively whipping my head around to see what happened. Kyle was standing there, his hands raised in a faux apologetic stance.

"Welcome to the Academy!" he snarled, laughing as he walked away. That was all the introduction I needed to know that Kyle Larson is an asshole—by nature and by choice.

Kyle's gears are turning, I can smell the burning, and he has that evil glint in his eye that makes my entire body freeze. An easy target.

"Ms. Walker, I have a question." He waves his hand in the air, playing the role of astute student, though I know better than to believe it. Ms. Walker, however, takes the bait and gives him the floor. "If what Alexandra is saying is true, and we make choices, and those choices control our future. Does that mean that she chose to kill her father?"

The air is sucked out of the room. A tremor builds in my hands, and I know I'm done for. Once that starts, there's no turning back. The tears spring to my eyes, pressing against the rims and threatening to spill over. I try to steady my breath, to tame the storm, but it's too late.

"Out, now." Ms. Walker points Kyle to the door, sending him to Headmaster Johnson's office. She's on her phone immediately, texting furiously, so she doesn't see that it's me who is moving, my feet retreating at a rapid pace. All I can think of is being anywhere but here. Those eyes burning into me, judging me, mocking me. My guilt a swirling tornado, sucking me in and blaming me for my father's death.

I burst out of the English classroom, my feet picking up speed as I tear down the hallway. The pressure behind my eyes grows, wet seeping out of the socket. The dam is about to burst, and the new girl can't be caught falling apart in the middle of the hallway. I'd never live that down. I dip into the closest bathroom, falling into the closest stall, and slam the door behind me. I climb up onto the toilet, my shoes braced on each side of the seat. I curl myself into a fetal ball, head between my legs to catch my breath.

I squeeze my eyes shut and try to remember Dr. Dave's instructions for when my body is falling out from under me, and I've lost all control. *Breathe*, he'd say. *Inhale, one, two three, exhale.*

Kyle may be a jerk, but he's not wrong. That's the part that hurts the most. I did kill my father. Not on purpose, but he's dead all the same. I'm no longer just parts, but barbed wire and broken glass stuffed in between. Because I was driving, so it's my fault. Not the deer's. Even though it looked me right in the eye as it jumped in front of the car. Even though I had no time to realize I shouldn't be able to see it that closely before I ran us right into its body. Even though it was an accident, it was still my fault.

I chose to get behind the wheel that day. I chose not to pay enough attention.

The door of my stall shakes, the looping handwriting on the wall that's much too pretty for the crude words it spells starts convulsing. The handle jiggles as two small, leather clad feet peek up at me from under the stall door. There is a quiet knock.

"Alexandra?" It's the soothing, welcome whisper of my friend Hannah. I met her my first week here, tucked into the heels of my other friend, Kayla. They are my saviors. The popular girls, plucking the new girl from nowhere and giving her immediate coveted status in the sea of students. Hannah's more on the shy side than exuberant Kayla, but she has this endearing habit of showing up out of nowhere every time I need her. "I heard what happened in English—are you okay?"

A snort escapes my nose, followed by a sniffle. I pull a wad of toilet paper from the dispenser and press it against my face. Blow. Toss it into the toilet and flush my sorrows away. Recomposed, I stretch out and unlock the stall door. Hannah immediately swings it open, a smile playing at her lips as she sees me—a gargoyle perched on the toilet seat. Just as frightening, no doubt.

"Who knew that the Nature vs Nurture debate would send me spiraling, huh?" I offer weakly, taking her extended hand and climbing down from my perch. Hannah disappears into her sweater, hiding behind her soft brown curls. The bangles lining her arms tinkle as she moves. The girl wears so many accessories, as if they'll somehow protect her. She pulls me out of the stall and leads me to the sink, faucets at the ready. But my reflection in the mirror catches me off guard.

Auburn hair falling from its plait. Mascara tears. Red blotches across my pale skin. I look like shit. But I can't stop staring at this image of myself. Who I've become, who this school is trying to make me.

Me: Seventeen. Favorite color: Pink. Favorite Singer: Taylor Swift. Favorite Book: *Little Women*.

I spent the summer in cute colorful dresses, listening to Kayla drone on about the Kardashians, or mostly, boys. I felt weightless and on top of the world.

But also me: Killer of father. Redeeming my future. Struggling to make my mother proud.

And I can't forget that no matter how hard I try.

When you have a near-death experience, your life is supposed to flash in front of your eyes. In my case, my life flashed in front of my mother's eyes. I spent three long months in the hospital under the watchful eye of doctors and the scratchy fabric of bandages as they pieced me back together. Then I was pushed out front in a wheelchair, my mother jumping out of our packed minivan to greet me and drag me here without a second thought. A fresh start.

"Here, some reinforcements?" Hannah offers me her makeup bag and the opportunity to touch up my now blotchy, mascara-streaked face. I paw through the case, pull out her mascara, find the gloss, and get to work.

My pale face stares back at me. Not long ago, it was a cross stitch of small scars from where shards of glass from the windshield sliced me open. When no matter what I did, I was a walking billboard for the worst day of my life. I figured I would have to live the rest of my days doused in foundation and cover up. But other than one small scar above my right eyebrow, the only marks left on me now are the ones you can't see.

My eyes meet Hannah's in the mirror. "Here, try a little liner," she offers, holding out a charcoal pencil.

"Yeah, no thanks. That's not really me," I shrug, to Hannah's disappointment. She and Kayla make themselves up on the reg but no matter how many YouTube tutorials I watch, it just doesn't feel natural. I can't get the hang of anything other than some basic mascara and a bit of lip gloss. Mom says that's all I need, anyway. That I'm beautiful just the way I am. Some days I even believe her.

Hannah stares at me for a beat, long enough to make me feel a little self-conscious. I avert my eyes, throw the make-up back in the case, and hand it back to her.

"You ready?" she asks, trying to instill confidence in me. I breathe it in, collect myself. Everyone will have heard about my outburst in class by now, the rumor mill hard at work, but what does it matter? What do these people matter? If I can make it through another year, I'll be graduating and can get the hell out of here.

# T W O

**THE PA SYSTEM SCREECHES** muffled words of wisdom I can't make out over sounds of the students in the hallway. The walls are caked with bright neon fliers, screaming:

Today is the first day of the rest of your life!

I still want to puke.

The Academy prides itself on reform. Bringing light to the dark. Changing the past for a better future. These fliers, their bright colors, are supposed to help eclipse our *before*. The lives we used to live. The things we did that brought us here.

It doesn't matter if they dress us up in proper blazers or try to wipe away our personal identities with rules and regulations. We will still scramble to cling to our former sense of selves. It's a battle of will. Because without the things that make us who we are, there's nothing left.

I trail Hannah as she weaves through the crowd, my shoulders knocking into someone every so often. Scowls find me, trying to make me shrink. Blake Andrews, adrenaline junkie caught drag racing with his dad's Tesla. Scowl. Sarah Daniels, actual junkie, jumping from rehab to rehab. Scowl. Drew Bailey brought a gun to school. Scowl.

There are never any whispers about Kayla and Hannah. I've never asked about their *before*, and they certainly never volunteered it. But Alexandra Shaw, she chose to kill her father.

Though despite what everyone thinks, that isn't why I'm here. This is a reform school, but I'm not here to be reformed. After the accident, we needed a fresh start. Mom was able to get a job here, which afforded her living arrangements and private school education for her daughter. But try telling that to the other kids—I swear, I'm not like you; I'm just here for the free education!

Laughter trails behind me, whispers just loud enough for me to hear. Their words hook into me. I know I need to brush them off. I need a thicker skin. But I'm still working on that. I'm alone in the sea of sharks circling the waters, hunting for fresh blood.

"Alexandra!" My name pierces through the hum, sounding far more regal than I could ever be on the posh tongue of Kayla. She's a beacon of safety in this shitstorm. Her blonde hair is slung casually over her shoulder, her sun-kissed skin practically glistening under the fluorescent lights. She's a model posing for a fashion shoot—all angles and sharp features.

My shoulders relax. My breath levels out. Kayla, my hero.

As students pass, they cower at her presence. Kimberly Marshall fumbles through the crowd with a Yearbook-issued giant camera. She hesitates as she nears us. I can tell she wants to ask us to pose for a photo but is too nervous to speak. Kayla challenges her with a raised eyebrow and Kimberly immediately backs away. I'm sure her assignment is to capture at least one photo of Kayla and her squad. But apparently failing that assignment seems less of a danger than bothering Pine Cliff's queen bee.

I don't know why Kayla chose to pull me up to her level. But she did. I was timidly walking through the front doors of this school on my first day. Head down, hair a mass of red chaos around my face to hide the fading scars from the accident. There were whispers about me. I could hear them hanging in the air. I was the girl who killed her father. They all knew it. Some people stared. People like Kyle lashed out. But not Kayla. Kayla came right up to me, brushed the hair behind my ears, and smiled.

*I like a girl who's been through some shit*, she said with her confident smile and a wink in her eye. I don't know what I would have done without her those first few weeks. She led me through the school each day, as if I already belonged. Stood over me, batting away their questions and inquisitive looks.

Because of her, I always had a seat in the cafeteria at lunch, an ear to confide in, and an ally to draw strength from. New students rarely have the advantage of a protector, let alone one with school status that puts them six feet above everyone else.

"So, did you hear Brian is having a party Friday night?" Kayla hasn't stopped talking since I met her. She's a ball of energy, always fluttering around us. She's how I know about all the school's gossip, about everyone's *before*. She carries people's secrets in her back pocket, locked and loaded.

She would have heard about my scene in English class by now, but she's too caught up in her own excitement to mention it. I choose to believe this is because she knows I'll be ok. That I don't need to be coddled. "Alexandra! A party? Andy is coming home with some of his uni mates and they're buying a keg."

Brian's brother Andy is an Academy alumnus, rather legendary among the rest of us living in his shadow. He's the Academy's success story, the poster child for their reform program. We've all seen his profile in the brochure. Heard how he knocked off some liquor store at thirteen and then his entire family up and moved to this nothing town. It's unusual for whole families to relocate. Usually, they ship their delinquent child off to board here. But Andy's family is an exception, forcing Brian to follow in his brother's footsteps whether he had a *before* or not. They live in an Academy appointed house not far from the school. Similar to my mother and me.

Andy graduated a couple of years ago and is studying at Carver, one of the elite universities that every parent wants their kids to go to. Brian has some big shoes to fill and as far as I can tell, he has nothing but small feet.

"You know what it's like when he comes back. Their parents let their guard down and their home turns into Disneyland. This party will be brilliant. More people, more opportunities... more mature boys..."

"Yo, is that all you ever think about? Boys?" On cue, Brian cuts into our conversation, pushing his way into our little huddle. Brian is basically that character from every '90s teen movie Kayla forced us to watch. You know the one with the goofy grin and the long, greasy hair. The one who skateboards to school and smokes weed out back between classes. Even with shorter hair and a uniform, he still has that slacker vibe about him.

"I only think about one boy, actually. You might know him, he looks a lot like you… only much, much better." Kayla retorts, though there's a flirtatious tone to her voice.

Brian feigns hurt, miming a knife to his heart. "One of these days, Kayla, I'll show you that you're better off with me than my idiot older brother."

Kayla laughs at the word idiot, as if it's the funniest thing she's ever heard. Hannah smothers a smirk with her hand, pulling her cardigan further over her fingers.

"You'll come though, right? To the party?" Brian turns to me and shoves a bright pink flier into my hand. Big bold letters across the top read:

ARE YOU ONE OF THEM

"What is this trash?" Kayla grabs the flier from my hand. "Are you one of who? What the hell is that supposed to mean?"

"Are you one of the cool kids invited to my party, duh," Brian answers proudly, and Kayla rolls her eyes again. He always tries to be so mysterious; pretending everything he does is part of a secret, exclusive club. Though he never quite pulls it off.

Kayla crumples it up and tosses it to me, just missing Hannah. I catch it somehow and shove it into my locker along with my bag, knocking out some of my books.

*Never Let Me Go* by Kazuo Ishiguro clatters to the floor, and Hannah immediately stoops down to grab it, almost protectively. She glances around as if she's scared someone saw the book being poorly treated. I forgot she had loaned it to me weeks ago, saying I *had* to read it, but I haven't.

Hannah's always giving me books to read. The last book she slipped into my locker was *The Bell Jar*. I was sure it'd be a drag, but it resonated with me in a way I didn't realize books could. Made me start to question who I was, who I wanted to be. I don't know where she finds these books—our library here is all academic texts, I've never seen anything like what she reads here.

I smile sheepishly, about to apologize, but Kayla cuts in again.

"Alexandra will be there, right?" Kayla looks at me, exasperated. "Alexandra, are you even listening to me?"

I still don't answer her as I try to focus on Hannah's expression. I expected her to be hurt, but there's something close to anger spreading across her face. Frustration. I am immediately guilty, though her reaction seems a little over the top. I try to focus. My line of sight is blurring, my head throbbing lightly behind my eyes. I blink them open and closed, open and closed.

The doctors told me the blurred vision was a residual issue from the head trauma of the accident and that it would go away with time. It's been six months, and nothing has changed.

"Alexandra?" Kayla tries again, shoving me with her shoulder.

"What? Yeah, whatever, I'll go," I mumble my response.

"Stubborn cow." Kayla says, flashing me her brilliant smile.

"Preppy priss," I respond, our little routine. Falling right in line.

I don't know if I will go to the party, but at least Kayla will bugger off for a few hours. She sashays away, the sea of students parting as she moves. The hallway a red carpet rolled out ahead of her treating her as the royalty she is. She skips past Ms. Walker and Headmaster Johnson at the end of the hall. His face is red, sweat glistening on his brow. She has her hands on her hips, her head tilted at a severe angle, full of attitude. They are standing with Mom, who looks less than impressed at being cornered in the hallway full of students. I rarely see her during school hours, even though she works here.

Kayla doesn't notice, but I do, and I worry that they're talking about me. Ms. Walker being scolded for how I behaved in her class. Mom being called and informed of my transgression. My old friend guilt reaches its gnarled fingers towards me, and I fight to bat it away.

As if on cue, they all turn to me. I slam my locker shut and take off down the hall, letting the crowd swallow me whole.

"Hey Hannah, wait up!" I call after her as she makes her way through the students. She stops, a soft smile on her lips. "What do you think of this party? Are you going to go?"

"I'm not sure it matters what I think of it. Kayla wants to go, so I'll be there. You should come too; it might be fun." She says the words, but I'm not sure she believes them.

"I mean, I'll think about it. But I'll have to ask my mom and you know what she's like…" I trail off when Hannah visibly bristles. She's spent a few afternoons at my house, but ever since my mother started working here, Hannah's been a little hesitant to come over. I never press her on it, but there's clearly more to this than Hannah lets on. Whether it's my mom specifically that makes her uncomfortable or mother figures in general.

"This is me," she says, stopping outside of her classroom. "Think about the party though, okay? I think it will be good for you."

"I will, definitely," I nod, breaking away from her, but she calls me back.

"Wait… I know it doesn't seem like a big deal, but I think you should read this." Hannah shoves her copy of *Never Let Me Go* into my hands. "I think you would like it," she says again.

"Okay, I promise I will. If it means that much to you." I take the book and shove it into my messenger bag.

Hannah offers me a weird smile that doesn't reach her eyes before dipping into her classroom.

# THREE

**THE REST OF THE** day goes by without issue and when school lets out, I take my usual long way home. I wander behind the Academy, leaving the monstrous stone building behind me. Gazing up at the oversized windows, the brooding gables, and the ivy that climbs up the wall and then just…. stops…. always makes me feel infinitely small. Too small to belong. But I guess none of us do, which is why we are here in the first place.

The Academy sits on a peninsula with its rear facing a cliff that looms over a cove of water below. There's a running track that takes up most of the grass and a stone wall that lines the cliff's edge. The wall stretches out towards a massive forest to the East where the trees are still covered in crisp green leaves with Fall just out of September's reach.

I follow the stone wall to the forest, pausing to watch the long, thin fingers or the sun stretch down between the branches.

Creatures titter in the trees above, sharing all their secrets. The smell of wildflowers lingers in the breeze. I make my way across a foot-worn bridge along a path that loops back out to the main road at the other end of my street. Between school and home, this is one of the few moments I have entirely to myself. I bask in that freedom as long as I can.

Mom is in the kitchen when I get home. I hear the distinctive sound of vegetables being chopped, but she can't hear me over the music she's listening to as I come in. I recognize the song; it's something my dad used to listen to when I was younger. He'd pick me up and twirl me around, his hand in mine as we danced. Mom would stand behind him, watching, laughing. I wonder if that song makes her think about this moment, too.

I'd ask her, but we don't talk about my dad. There are no pictures of him in our new place. We don't reminisce about my childhood memories or how things used to be, *before*. Mom pretends he doesn't exist, that he never did. But I think about him every single day. Think about what I did. Every. Single. Day.

It's taken us a long time to get to where we are. That is, a state where Mom doesn't seem to outwardly blame me for losing her husband. For a while, I was sure she'd never forgive me, her resentment a dark cloud following me everywhere. But we spent months in therapy, repairing our relationship. Making promises that we would do our best for each other. That I would do my best at school and show her how far I've come, and how far I can go. To make her proud.

I still see our therapist, Dr. Dave. It was part of the deal. They monitor me as if I'm some kind of criminal and this school is the prison. Depending on who you ask, I guess it is a prison. Depending on who you ask, I guess I am a criminal, too.

Moving here and starting over was a blank slate, a chance for us to mend our relationship and move forward without the past dragging us down. And it's worked so far. We're in a good place. As long as I continue to keep my head down and focus on school, the waters are calm.

I close the front door and shatter her reverie. She startles, as if I caught her sneaking a cigarette, though she's never smoked. We share an awkward stare for a beat too long before a smile takes over and she greets me warmly.

"Alexandra, how was your day?" She places the knife down on the chopping block, giving me her full attention. Her eyes bore into mine, open, expectant. I try to look for the clouds behind them; they're clear.

"It was fine, same as always. Another day with Pine Cliff's best!" I answer. A little more sarcastically than intended, but I still feel shaken after my encounter with Kyle Larson this morning.

Her brows crease and she stares at me until I regret my tone.

"I'm sorry. I'm just in a mood. How are you?" I wave my white flag, but I sincerely want to know. We'd always been able to talk to each other. Just sit and enjoy each other's company, talk for hours about school, life, and dreams. I want to fill our house with that same laughter and love so we can try to ignore the giant father-sized hole.

"Are you sure you're okay? You seem… preoccupied. Did

something happen at school?" There's a subtle edge to her voice and I know now that Headmaster Johnson and Ms. Walker *were* talking about me. That Mom knows everything about me running out of class this morning.

"It was nothing," I respond, heading for the stairs before she can ask me more about it.

"It didn't sound like nothing. You left class in the middle of a presentation? That's not like you. What happened?"

My foot hovers over the bottom step. I could keep going, pretend I didn't hear her. Just walk up to my room and avoid talking about this. The muscles in my leg twitch, edging me forward, but I can't bring myself to take the step. Mom waits, opening herself up to me and I owe it to her to meet her halfway.

"Kyle Larson is what happened," I scoff, kicking my foot against the step and turning back towards the kitchen. "He made some comment about Dad, and I just couldn't deal with it. I lost my cool and had to leave."

Mom's face is unreadable. Like I said, we don't talk about my dad, so bringing him up casually in conversation is dangerous. I don't know how she will respond. I don't know if it will push her back into her shell. We've worked so hard to get to this good place; I don't want to ruin it. But she asked.

"Well, that boy has always been trouble. Did you know he got kicked out of his old school for hazing another student? A freshman on the football team," she responds, her shoulders relaxing just a bit as she picks up the knife to start chopping again. "I ought to talk to Headmaster Johnson about him…" The last part she says more under her breath than to me.

"Honestly, it was nothing. I just wasn't in the mood for him." I turn again, hoping this conversation is done, but Mom's voice pulls me back.

"Are you sure that's all?" Her voice is strained. She's struggling to keep it light and friendly. Her shoulders tense again.

I've always been the one to follow the rules, never to cause trouble. Especially these days. The last thing I want to do is cause more trouble, but I can't help myself. "I just can't stop thinking about Dad."

This makes Mom pause mid chop. "Your father loved music, you know." She starts, but she won't meet my eyes. Maybe she *was* thinking of him earlier before I interrupted. "He always had songs stuck in his head. Was always wandering around humming. It used to drive me crazy. But I miss that constant background noise. Everything is so quiet now." She smiles, a little sadly, and my heart swells. We never connect like this, not over my dad.

"Did Dad…" I want to ask more about him, take advantage of this open moment, but I trail off when I see her shoulders tense. I've already caused her enough pain, reliving these little moments. "Never mind, it doesn't matter."

I start to unload my messenger bag, placing textbooks and notebooks on the hall table. I pull out the book Hannah loaned me, inspecting it as if it holds all of life's answers.

"What's that?" Mom puts down the knife and walks around the kitchen island. Her voice comes out unnaturally high, a weird contrast to the heaviness of the question. Her attention falls more on the book than me. Her lemon scent surrounds me as she gets closer and something inside me stirs. My stomach clenches.

"Just a book Hannah gave me." I say flippantly, though I can't miss the way it makes my mother bristle.

"May I?" She plucks the book from my hands before I can even offer it to her.

"Have you read it?" I ask, hoping that it's an opportunity for us to bond and the uneasiness in my gut is not a strange warning.

"Is it on your curriculum?" she asks instead, flipping the book over and reading the back.

"No, not really. Hannah just thought I'd like it. Find it inspiring. She's always giving me books to read. And Ms. Walker doesn't seem to mind if we're reading other books in class as long as we finish the assignments." The words slip out before I realize the danger in them. My mother looms over me, her shoulders rigid, making my words mean more than they should. I'm clearly missing something.

"Ms. Walker should know better than to stray from the curriculum. There are rules for a reason." She huffs, clearly annoyed.

"It's not a big deal…" I try, but she cuts me off.

"You can't afford to fall behind on your actual schoolwork. You don't have time for books like this. I'll hold on to this for the time being."

"But it's not mine. Let me at least give it back to Hannah." I reach for the book, but she pulls it away from me.

"I'll see that it ends up where it belongs."

"Yeah, sure, alright..." I give her a tight smile and head towards the staircase.

"Alexandra?" she calls after me and I pause, my hand on the railing. "You know I only want what is best for you, right? That I'm just looking out for you?"

Her sincerity cracks through the wall I have built up and it crumbles slightly.

"I know," I answer weakly.

"It's been a tough year. For us both. I just want you to know that I'm trying."

"I know," I say again. "I'm trying too."

"I know honey. I love you," she says and a warmth flows through me.

"I love you too," I answer, meaning it.

# FOUR

**I DON'T KNOW HOW** I ended up in a computer programming class. I'm fairly sure it was a mistake on my schedule, and I thought about fixing it, but I couldn't be bothered. Though this morning, instead of perfecting my line of website code, I'm trying to find the SparksNotes version of that book Hannah loaned me.

I still can't shake her reaction, the way she protectively scooped it off the ground and as if I'd just told her that her favorite author died. Nor can I forget the way my mother reacted when she saw it. What is the big deal about this book? I ask the Internet, but the connection sucks and all my search results turn up nothing. As if the stupid book doesn't exist.

There's a loud thump from across the room. Kyle Larson, in all his douchebag glory, stands next to a row of computers beside another boy named Scott. Scott's chin-length dirty-blond hair falls over his face as he hunches over his computer keyboard. He's wearing a baggy black hoodie—cuffs frayed along the edges—which looks ridiculous under his school blazer. His entire look is against our dress code, but he's Headmaster Johnson's son, so no one will do anything about it.

Despite his father's best efforts, Scott is the kind of guy who has no problem spending an entire weekend in his basement in front of a computer screen or video game screen. Really any screen that offers a digital world for him to escape to will do.

Scott's head is full of other worlds to escape to. He writes stories about them and posts them online. Stories about robot women and lonely human boys. About computer nerds who rise up and save the world. I know this because Kyle found one recently and hasn't stopped throwing it in Scott's face.

"I read your story. Trashy sci-fi fan fiction." He's taunting him, waving around some pieces of paper. "Can't get yourself a real girlfriend, so you have to write them? Even these make-believe girls would want nothing to do with you. You know that, right?"

Some students chuckle. Scott's neck burns red. I keep my eyes glued to the screen in front of me. If there's one thing I've learned during my few months here, it's to mind my own business or be caught in the crossfire.

Besides, the school is supposed to discipline students. That's the whole point of this place. Their methods are a mystery, but students whisper about what happens behind closed doors. About tunnels and solitary rooms in the basement. About students disappearing for days at a time. I doubt there's any truth to them, but right now, I hope there is.

"Mr. Larson, sit down." Mr. Morrison finally decides to step into his authoritative role, hardly looking away from the whiteboard.

As he settles into his lesson, Kyle shifts in and out of the corner of my eye. He's glaring at Scott, flicking him incessantly in the ear. I wonder what makes someone so cruel. Did something happen to him as a kid? Is he riddled with insecurities and pent-up testosterone? Or is it something he was born with?

I'll tell you one thing; no matter how many schools they send him to, no matter how many proper blazers they dress him in, he will forever be an asshole.

When the bell rings, I hurry from the classroom, giving Kyle Larson as wide of a berth as I can. I can't handle another run in with him today. Even though Phys-Ed is my next class and I hate it with a passion, I can't get there soon enough.

The locker room is full of girls in various stages of undress when I burst in. I change quickly and then join our class outside on the track behind our school. I jog across the freshly cut grass to Kayla and Hannah as they idly walk along one of the chalked lanes. Kayla is scrolling mindlessly on her phone, Hannah walking quietly beside her.

"Hey," I breathlessly call as I catch up to them.

"Hey," Kayla doesn't even look up from her phone.

"Hi," Hannah at least looks at me, though her eyes seem to look through me.

Students jog past us, kicking up dirt in their wake. Kayla

coughs, waving her hands around to clear the air. Kimberly Marshall is standing at the sidelines watching the scene, her Yearbook camera *click, click, clicking.* Her get out of gym free card.

"Twats!" Kayla calls to the girls running by, stuffing her phone in her gym shorts pocket, and turning to me. "So, the party Friday is going to be pretty rad. Remember the last party they threw? Andy's going away party? It was epic."

"Epic is one way of putting it," Hannah mumbles, which provokes a glare from Kayla that I don't miss.

"What do you mean?" I ask innocently.

"Oh, you haven't heard?" Kayla fakes surprise. Of course, I haven't heard. If they haven't told me, no one else would have. My interest has inadvertently given Kayla the stage she's been looking for and she stops walking, pulling me in close as if she's sharing a secret. "Well, Andy's graduating class was having a party on the beach below the cliffs. Bonfire blazing, moon high and bright, so bright they didn't need to use flashlights. Out of nowhere, a shrill cry pierced the air and everyone at the party froze, looking around, wondering where it came from. Someone started yelling and pointing up at the cliff and everyone rushed closer to the bottom for a better view."

I'm a sucker for Kayla's storytelling, but Hannah rolls her eyes at the drama of it all. I wonder how many times she's heard this story. I swat at her, motioning for Kayla to continue.

"Perched on the edge was a girl named Emily Tran. She was like a ghost, floating on top of that cliff. Her white nightgown billowing around her in the wind. Her long dark hair in a braid hanging over one shoulder. Bellowing out a string of ear-piercing shrieks, something between a laugh and a cry. Everyone froze in terror, not sure what to do, mouths wide, watching."

My mouth is hanging open too, waiting. Kayla basks in my attention, drags out the suspense, enjoying every moment. Completely ignoring Hannah's impatient toe tapping.

"With the crowd of seniors as her witness, Emily raised her arms and swan dove off the cliff onto the stretch below. Her body splayed among the rocks; unnatural angles, elbows and limbs entangled. Her hair ripped from her braid, left to cascade around her in the current, tangling with the slimy weeds like a creature of the sea. A blanket of crimson cloaked the shore, bright and sticky in the moonlight." Kayla looks triumphant. In all her glory sharing gossip to virgin ears.

"That's horrible!" I gasp, the haunting story painting a vivid image in my mind. "Were you there?"

"No, but Andy told me *everything*," she smiles dreamily. "There are so many stories like this. Most about students who have some kind of meltdown in the hallways or at a school dance, cause a big scene and are whisked away. Then they reappear a few weeks later as if nothing happened. But some, every so often, flee to the cliffs and jump." Kayla whispers this as if she's telling me a ghost story around a campfire.

The cliffs to the north of the track we're walking on seem far more eerie now that they're put in this different context. I look to Hannah for confirmation, hoping Kayla is just trying to scare me.

But Hannah's expression is dead serious, and I know this is no joke.

"She 'went wild.' That's what we call it. It doesn't happen often, but every graduating year has its own urban legend. Someone who knew someone who seemed completely fine, just 'goes wild'." Hannah adds and despite the sun's warmth, a shiver runs down my spine.

We walk in silence for a few minutes, slowly making our way around the track. I can't shake the story. It's another one to add to the list of rumors and strange things about this school.

"Hannah!" a voice calls out across the track. The three of us look over at Ms. Walker standing by the gym door, her expression distraught. Hannah picks up into an actual jog and cuts across the field to her. We both follow.

"What's going on?" Kayla is the one to question through gasping breaths. Ms. Walker barely registers her, her eyes focused only on Hannah.

"Headmaster Johnson is raiding your locker," Ms. Walker shares and Hannah immediately pales. "I tried to explain how unreasonable and ridiculous that is. That you of all students wouldn't be harboring anything worth searching for. But he said he received a tip from a reliable source that you were hoarding and sharing contraband items."

Ms. Walker's eyes flit to me as she says this, and my stomach drops out. Does she think I'm somehow responsible for this? That I tipped Headmaster Johnson off? I don't have the chance to defend myself as Hannah speaks up.

"It's okay, they won't find anything." She says it with confidence. Like there was something to find, and it's no longer there. Ms. Walker visibly relaxes.

"What a crock. As if Hannah would have anything to do with drugs. That's completely bonkers. If anything, they should be raiding my locker!" Kayla is idly chatting away as she leads us back towards the change room, but no one is listening.

Hannah and Ms. Walker share a look I can't decipher before Hannah follows her into the building as well.

"Alexandra?" Ms. Walker places a gentle hand on my arm to stop me. "You'll keep an eye out for her, won't you? Hannah?"

Her words take me by surprise. If they found nothing in her locker, this will all be a misunderstanding, not something that Hannah needs to worry about. I don't see how me keeping an eye out for her will do anything, but I nod anyway.

"Of course, not a problem." I answer with a fake smile before disappearing into the depths of the school.

# FIVE

**I TAKE LONGER THAN** usual getting myself together after gym and the cafeteria is crowded when I arrive, but Kayla and Hannah are already sitting in our spot. Because of Kayla, we sit closer to the windows with the popular students, away from the garbage cans and the dish drop. Spoiler alert: even when you dress everyone in the same uniforms and dictate their everyday routines, they will still carve out a hierarchy. The cool kids still rise to the top. Oil and water.

I grab a green tray from the rack at the front of the cafeteria and step into the lunch line. We all have the pleasure of being registered for a standard meal plan. Every student and teacher is served their choice of limp sandwich or hot meal, accompanied by our very own Pine Cliff Cola. If that doesn't sound appetizing... it's because it's not.

Everything smells of olive oil and dirt, no matter what it is.

Today's menu is stringy spaghetti with meatballs, though the students have an ongoing bet about what meat these balls are actually made of. My stomach roils at the thought, though the feeling may also be attributed to the boy standing three heads in front of me.

Kyle Larson's leaning his hairy arms against the display counter standing between the kitchen staff and us. His weasel eyes have narrowed in on the chef.

"So, Carol—is today the day you're finally going to tell us what, exactly, you grind into these meatballs?" The smirk he wears is similar to the one that cut across his smug face when he called me out in class the other morning. I want nothing more than to slap it off him. An urge that is out of character for me, but one I'm happy to embrace.

"As I've told you, Mr. Larson, they are made from the remains of annoying Academy boys who didn't know how to keep their mouths shut and appreciate the food that is being offered to them," Carol retorts and it's my turn to smirk.

"I wonder how Headmaster Johnson would feel if he knew how you spoke to his students?" Kyle offers, standing victoriously against the display case.

"I'd like to see him find a replacement who can put up with you lot on a daily basis. Here," Carol takes an overflowing dish of spaghetti and places it on Kyle's tray. She tops it off with a heaping spoonful of meatballs. "Enjoy your friends." She doesn't smile as she pushes his tray further down the line before turning to Kimberly Marshall.

Their interaction is much less dramatic, Kimberly's mousy nervousness sealing her mouth shut as she fiddles with the ligatures on the giant camera hanging around her neck. She keeps glancing at me out of the corner of her eye and I can't tell whether she wants to say something, or she's scared of me. She quickly accepts the lunch offering with only a subtle nose crinkle and hurries from the kitchen area to her designated seat not far from the dish drop.

When I approach, Carol's face finally softens. "Alexandra, the usual?" she asks, and I nod.

"I don't know how you put up with us day in and day out," I say. I put my tray up on the counter so she can place the empty bowl on top. She fills it with a puddle of watery spaghetti, but instead of topping it with suspicious meatballs, she reaches under the counter and pulls out a secret stash of Parmesan cheese. This she reserves for the students who don't give her a hard time.

"It's amazing what you can do when you have to. The things you'll put up with when you have no other choice." Carol fiddles with some of the serving spoons resting on the counter in front of her, not meeting my eyes. There's a long pause.

"Oh, I'll take a Cola too, please," I break the silence and she looks up at me quickly. Her eyebrows pull tight as her lips pucker.

"Are you sure? You know Cola isn't good for you…." She trails off, a shadow falling across her face.

"As if any of this food is?" I smile as she heads back to the Cola machine. It sputters to life as she places the cup underneath the spout waiting for the sticky sweet liquid to pour out. She places it onto my tray and pushes it down the line, a little too abruptly. Some of the Cola escapes through the straw hole in the lid.

"Take care of yourself, Alexandra." The way her voice dips makes her sentiment more of a warning than a casual departure.

I follow the line of students out of the serving area and head towards the back of the room. Past Ms. Walker reading at a table near the garbage cans. Past Kimberly Marshall, who is sharing a table with only her camera and sitting facing our table, stealing glances any chance she can. Past the other students who are weirdly zombie-like, sipping on their Colas and twirling their spaghetti.

I have barely even taken a seat at our table when Kayla shoves her phone in front of my face.

"Alexandra, will you look at this? Tell me this isn't the most perfect specimen?" She's waving the phone around erratically. I grab it, peering at the screen. She has her Instagram open, but it's not her profile. "Don't you think Andy is even more handsome now that he's a college man?" Her voice dips into a dreamy tone, and she audibly sighs.

"Yeah, he's alright." And he is. Andy is handsome in that blond-haired, chiseled tan body, surfer dude kind of way, if that's your thing. And it is clearly Kayla's thing. She and Andy have a past. One that expired long before I got here, one that hasn't existed since Andy left, but one that Kayla seems determined to reignite at the party.

"Alright? Are you daft? Look at that golden god. Hannah, don't you agree?" She asks, pushing the phone towards Hannah.

She's lost in thought, her eyes focused on Ms. Walker, who never had a hope for a better seat, being on lunch duty and all. Ms. Walker always brown bags her lunch, even though teachers are offered the same meal plan, and she always has a water bottle that she's sipping from. Like with the meatballs, students take bets on what is actually in the bottle. If it were me, it'd be something strong.

"Hannah!"

"What?" Hannah draws her eyes back to us, then down at the phone pointedly. "He's not my type, Kayla." She shifts her gaze to the sandwich on her tray, unwrapped but untouched. Hannah rarely touches her food, usually just pushes it around. A red flag. I worry she's intentionally not eating and what that means, whether I need to ask.

It's not that I'm observant enough to notice Hannah's potential eating disorder. The cafeteria is lined with bulletin boards. Pull-tabs for self-help groups. Checklists of what to look for in other students. Signs of depression, angst, and suicidal thoughts. I've read all the fliers.

How to be happy!
Don't lose who you are!
Is your best friend struggling?

And I think my best friend is struggling. It's not the first time I've wondered about Hannah's *before*. What her parents thought was worth plucking her out of her life and shipping her across the country to this place. Restrictive eating? Or maybe it's more than that.

Kayla doesn't notice. She never notices. She huffs, leaning back in her chair pouting. As if Hannah owed it to her to at least pretend to care about her current obsession.

"Are you okay?" I ask Hannah, who obviously is not okay. Kayla shoots me a look that looks purely annoyed that I'm giving my energy to my other friend instead of her. "Did they raid your locker? What were they looking for?"

"Books," Hannah answers simply.

"Books?" I ask, confused. "This is a school. What else do they think is going to be in your locker? That doesn't make sense."

"Not textbooks, other books. That aren't on our curriculum or in our library." She answers and guilt seeps into my stomach. Of course. My mom saw the book Hannah loaned me, acted so weird, and then Hannah's locker was raided. That's no coincidence. But why would she do that?

I'm about to ask, but Kimberly Marshall, hovering at the end of our table, lets out a little cough. I didn't notice her leave the safety of her end of the cafeteria and approach. She looks nauseous as she waits for an opening, her Yearbook camera held carefully in her hands.

"Uh, hi guys!" she interrupts with a confident perkiness that is clearly an act. "Mind if I take your photo? For the yearbook?"

Kayla turns her head towards Kimberly, intentionally slow to drag out the moment. To leave her hanging there anticipating the reaction. I'm anticipating it too. I can't tell whether Kayla will be friendly and receptive or tell her to go shove her camera where it hurts. Kimberly wobbles back and forth on her feet, trying her hardest not to run away.

"I suppose you wouldn't have much of a yearbook without a photo of us, would you?" Kayla finally answers, an air of indifference around her.

"No, definitely not. You guys were my priority today. If I can secure this photo, the whole spread will be designed around you three." Kimberly is blushing as she admits this, and Kyla doesn't miss a beat.

"Is that why you have been stalking us through the halls all week? Lurking around corners, ready to pounce and then always chickening out?"

Kimberly blushes again, adjusting her collar and clearing her throat. "I mean, I was just, I had to wait for the right time..." she stammers, and Kayla looks satisfied.

"Ignore her," Hannah cuts in and Kayla cuts her an annoyed look. "We would be happy to pose for you. Alexandra, scooch in." Hannah gestures for me to pull in closer and she drapes her arms around Kayla and me, pulling us in tight.

Kimberly fiddles with her camera, adjusting the lens, and takes a few steps back to frame the shot.

"Chop, chop!" Kayla snaps. Kimberly's finger finds the button and she takes a flurry of photos as the three of us give our best model poses. Puckering our lips, jutting out our hips, poofing up our hair. When Kayla has enough, she pushes us away.

"You're welcome," she smirks at Kimberly. "Make sure to tell your classmates how accommodating we were."

Kimberly nods and quickly retreats. I roll my eyes.

"What, you have a problem with me?" Kayla asks, catching my reaction. My heart skips a beat, her narrowed eyes assessing me.

"No, definitely not. But I mean, she's just trying to do her job. You don't have to give everyone such a hard time." I try to back pedal.

"Easy for you to say, from your place at the top of the castle," Kayla scoffs, standing. "I have better things to do than sit here and be judged by you. I'll catch you two later." She pushes her lunch tray across the table and sashays out of the cafeteria.

This tension between us is new. I'm not sure what changed, but every time I open my mouth, I seem to offend Kayla. Hannah offers me a small reassuring smile, but it doesn't help me feel better and I turn back to my lukewarm lunch.

I twirl my spaghetti around my fork. It slurps through the sauce, a hypnotizing rhythm. Turning and turning and turning… and then the table tilts. Morphing from the laminate cafeteria table into a white tablecloth. The hum of student chatter around me turns into the soft sound of classical music tinkling in the background of a dimly lit restaurant. My fork is still full of spaghetti, but the colors are richer, not watered-down cafeteria food, but something classier.

*An Italian restaurant. A basket full of bread sticks. I'm smiling, laughing. Feeling entirely at ease. And I'm not alone. There's a stranger across from me, dark hair falling into green-gray eyes. Strong arms cross against his chest. I'm fixated on a line of ink that runs along his forearm, trying to make out the shape of the tattoo. He leans back in his chair, showing off, when the legs go right out from under him. He falls, sprawled on the floor in the middle of that restaurant. Red as a beet. But the embarrassment only lasts a minute and then he rights himself, and all feels right in the world.*

I nearly choke on my spaghetti. Hannah's voice cuts into the quiet music, tearing me back to myself.

"Alexandra, are you okay?" She thumps me on the back, too hard. I cough and a strand of spaghetti shoots out of my mouth and onto the table in front of us. We both stare at it.

"Went down the wrong tube," I choke out. My eyes water, my throat burns and my head pounds, a pressure building behind my eyes.

The doctors commented on this. Moments of confusion, thoughts jumbled up from the accident. But this was more than just jumbled thoughts. I was here, and then suddenly I was somewhere else. With someone else. A strange boy. Though it all felt familiar. He felt familiar. Déjà vu, but not.

What the hell just happened?

# S I X

**I'M SURE I HAVE** afternoon classes, but the only thing I can focus on is what happened in the cafeteria. Or what I think happened because I definitely have no idea what that was.

An Italian restaurant. A boy. A date.

Definitely a date. But… I don't date. I haven't dated. Any girl will tell you this school is practically undateable. So what, then. A fantasy? A daydream? But it felt so real.

Maybe I crossed over to another dimension?

"Alexandra," the impatient voice of my teacher cuts into my thoughts. "You seem entirely engaged, so you must know the answer to this problem?" he points to a math problem on the white board, knowing that I am absolutely not engaged.

My face flushes. Math is not my strong suit.

"One hundred and seventeen." Comes a tiny whisper from behind me.

"One hundred and seventeen." I call out immediately, not even pausing to think if it even makes sense. And according to the lopsided frown on my teacher's face, it doesn't.

There are muffled chuckles as I sink further into my chair.

"Anyone else?" He looks around the room.

"Seventy-five," Kimberly Marshall's voice rings out behind me. Loud and confident. But there is no mistaking that voice, the same one that whispered the wrong answer into my ear.

I whip around in my chair and glare at her. Satisfied and proud of herself. What did I ever do to her?

"Wrong move, Marshall." Kayla leans over from the next row, her teeth bared. Kimberly goes stiff, eyes locked on the board in front of us. My body relaxes. Kayla, my protector, strikes again.

I try to pay more attention as the lesson continues, but the distractions keep coming. I can't stop thinking of that boy. Of the tattoo that ran up his arm. It was black and clearly had a design to it, but I didn't see it clear enough to make it out.

A wad of crumpled up paper bounces lazily off the back of my head. It could be another trap, another opportunity to make fun of the new girl, but I bend down to grab it anyway. Smoothing out the page until there are loopy, perfectly handwritten letters laid out before me.

*Whatsup with u?*

Kayla's handwriting. I glance over my shoulder to her watching me. She gestures to the note, telling me to write back. But how much time do we have? Writing out what's going on with me will take more than this one piece of paper. It will take hours of discussion and analyzation and maybe even some medical professionals.

????????

Is what I end up with, tossing the crumpled ball over my shoulder onto Kayla's desk across the aisle. I don't need to look behind me to feel the disappointment coming off her in waves. Definitely not the answer she was hoping for. But it sums up exactly whatsup with me. I don't know.

A moment later, there's a tiny clonk on my shoulder again. The paper thrown back. I quickly grab it and unravel it.

*Brian's party Friday night will make it better.*

No questions, no other concerns. Just another step to her end goal. Brian's party.

I don't bother to write back, scrunching up the paper in my fist and tossing it into my bag. There's a dramatic sigh from behind me, but surprisingly, I don't seem to care about disappointing her. For once, Kayla's not the main focus of my day.

That boy is.

🌲🌲🌲🌲

The trees are haunted.

Okay, they aren't literally haunted, but they may as well be. I can't take two steps on my usual route home without being reminded of that eerie tattoo from my vision in the cafeteria.

Vision.

That's what I'm calling it because it's not a dream—I was awake. Or a memory—I didn't recognize anything. Or déjà vu—wouldn't that mean I knew the boy? And I definitely don't know that boy. I would remember a boy like that.

The tattoo snapped into focus the minute I stepped into the forest. It was a line of trees running up along his arm. As clear as the trees in this forest. And the further I walk, the more each tree pokes me, running its branch fingers along my arm, unraveling more and more visions.

*A muscular arm brushing up to the side of my face.*

*A hand slowly tucking my auburn hair behind my ear.*

*Welcomed heat where his skin touches mine.*

I practically run through the woods the whole way home, trying to shake the visions. I burst through our front door to my mother sitting on the couch surrounded by papers. She looks up, slightly annoyed at the interruption, but quickly masks her reaction.

"Alexandra, are you okay? You seem out of breath. Did you run home?" she asks, as if the idea of me running is the most ridiculous thing she's heard all day.

"Did you tell Headmaster Johnson to search Hannah's locker?" I accuse, struggling to catch my breath. I throw my bag down at the front door and stomp toward the couch so that I'm towering over her.

"What are you talking about?" she says immediately, almost as if she were expecting this.

"They raided Hannah's locker today, looking for books that aren't part of our curriculum. Since when is it illegal to read books? Why would you do that?" I'm sweating, flustered. I want nothing more than for her to tell me I'm wrong, but when she does, I don't believe her.

"Honey, I really don't know what you're talking about. Here, sit." She pats the empty couch beside her. "You're all worked up. Tell me what this is all about."

"Honestly, it's been a weird day. A weird week. Forget it." I turn to leave the room, but Mom's voice pulls me back.

"Weird how?" She strains, struggling to keep it light and friendly. Her shoulders tense again.

"I've just… I don't even know how to explain it. I've been having this weird déjà vu? Just small things, flashes of places and people?" I trail off, sucking in my breath and holding it. Mom is going to think I'm losing my mind.

"Flashes of people?" She asks, her eyes narrowing slightly as she reaches for the glass on the table so her hands have something to hold to steady themselves.

The more I replay things in my mind, the more I see the boy and his tree tattoo, the more I'm convinced that I know it. But there was no face. As hard as I try to shift my mind's eye up, I can't focus on anything else. Because I don't know him, obviously. This stranger from my visions. How can I put a face to a boy I've never met?

"Alexandra, are you okay?" Mom asks again, and I realize I haven't given her any answers; I've just lost myself in my head.

I flush. "It's nothing. I think I'm just overtired."

"You have had a lot of catch up to do, starting last year so far into the semester. You've been working so hard. It sounds like everything is catching up to you." Her words cut through the tension in the air, and I can breathe again.

"Yeah, you're right. That's what it is. I think I'll go rest," I say, turning quickly and taking off towards my room.

"You are nothing, can't you see that?" Her voice stops me dead in my tracks.

"What?" I stutter, my heart beating a little faster. Did I hear that right? *You are nothing*.

"I said dinner's in twenty, you okay with that?" She watches the confusion spread over my face. "Are you sure you're okay? Did you hear me?"

I mumble a response, my voice caught up in my thoughts. Did I mishear, or did she know exactly what she was saying? I have no effing idea. I kick off my shoes and head up to my room, slamming the door behind me.

I throw my bag onto the floor and flop down on my bed. Fire flares in me. I am so angry. So angry, but I'm not even sure why. Kayla would laugh and flippantly say something about redheads and their tempers. But this is more than a short fuse.

I grab my phone, tap into my girls WhatsApp chat and start typing furiously:

**Alexandra**
I'm having such a weird night.

**Kayla**
Sounds rite for u

**Hannah**
What happened?

**Alexandra**
I don't know how to explain it without
sounding like I'm losing it.

**Kayla**
U already lost it

**Hannah**
Try? I might be able to help?

**Alexandra**
Well, my mom, for one. She was…
almost mean? Not outright, but passive
aggressively mean. Comments under
her breath, judgmental glares. We've
worked so hard to move past the
accident, I'm not sure where this is
coming from.

**Kayla**
Ur mum sux

**Hannah**
What she means is that your mom has always
been tough on you. You've just felt so guilty about
what has happened that you put up with it.
It sounds like you are tired of putting up with it.

I grip the phone tightly. Has my mother always done this? I think I would notice the sly comments. She's always been stubborn and strict, but supportive and looking out for my best interest. I'm not sure I see what they are talking about.

**Alexandra**:
It was weird. And not just her,
but I kept having these…
visions?

**Kayla**
Tell me the lotto #s, bitch

**Hannah**
What are you seeing?

                        **Alexandra**
                        A boy…

**Kayla**
Alexandra wants the D!

Hannah is typing…

**Kayla**
Ugh, I'm bored! I'm out. L8R, whores.

                        **Alexandra**
                        see you tomorrow.

I toss my phone onto the bed, blood bubbling in my veins. This is typical Kayla, but she's starting to piss me off. I've always just been happy to be in the same vicinity as her, grateful for what she's done for me. But lately, she's borderline insufferable.

I guess my mom's not the only one I'm tired of putting up with.

# SEVEN

**THE NEXT MORNING, I** do the usual zombie walk through the quiet streets towards the Academy. Dragging my feet. Stalling, where I can. When I see Kayla and Hannah waiting for me at the front gates as they always do, a weight lifts off my shoulders. I settle back into myself.

Something normal, and I need that sense of normalcy this morning.

"Alright?" Kayla asks, eyebrows pulling tightly together. She doesn't give any hint she's sorry for the way she derailed our conversation last night, not that I expected anything else. But I won't make it a thing; I just want to get on with the day.

"Yeah, sure… I didn't sleep very well last night." I mumble, taking the lead up towards the school with one friend on each side. Kayla walks like she owns the school, which I guess she kind of does. Head high, not bothering to cast anyone a simple glance.

But I notice them. The eyes that are on us as we walk three across the pathway to the school. We may as well be walking in slow motion, making a grand entrance. It doesn't usually bother me, but today I'd rather disappear into the background. I feel too much on display.

Hannah doesn't say anything, but she's pulling me apart with one look. She seems on edge. I can tell she wants to say something, but the moment is lost as Kayla pushes past us and heads into the school. Hannah follows her, giving me one last side-glance as I veer off in the opposite direction towards my first class. Life Studies.

In theory, this should be the one class that actually helps us prepare for, like, life. In practice, it's a joke. A class that acts as guidance counselor since the school itself won't splurge for one. It's the duty of all teachers to guide our students, not just one person, apparently.

Ms. Walker has been roped into leading Life Studies on top of English. She's young and cool so the school thinks the students will listen to her. Which is a crock of shit, obviously. Doesn't matter who you put in front of our future; the kids here will never see past their own present.

Ms. Walker is at her desk when I walk in, fumbling with a binder for today's lesson. She offers me a smile that isn't just a greeting, but an invitation. I want to apologize to her; that heated discussion with Headmaster Johnson the other morning, her pulling me aside after gym class. I didn't notice it then, but she looks to have sprung a leak. All the inspiration has drained out of her. She is the only teacher at this school who seems to care, and because I couldn't keep my shit together, she was talked down to.

"Hey, uh, about the other morning…" I trail off, hoping she'll catch my drift. Her dark eyes stare back at me from behind her thick frames, waiting for me to continue. "I'm sorry. I mean, if you got in trouble? For me leaving class? I saw Headmaster Johnson and my mom talking to you in the hallway, I just… I'm sorry."

Ms. Walker laughs. A full bodied, boisterous laugh, which surprises me. "I can handle Headmaster Johnson; don't you worry about me. I'm more concerned about you." A rock falls into my empty stomach. It's a trap. I try to unload some guilt and I've opened the door for a conversation.

"Oh, I'm fine. You don't have to worry about me either…" She's not buying it, her mouth pulled tightly, eyebrows raised. She turns back to her desk and pulls out some papers, handing me the top one. It's our last assignment. Questions and answers about what we want to be when we grow up. #LifeGoals.

"I found your Future Framework Assignment rather… interesting." She holds out the paper. My name scrawled at the top, a lot of empty space under the questions below. The entire paper is framed in smudged pencil doodles. "If you spent as much time thinking about your future as you do drawing in the margins, we might have something to work towards here."

"Maybe I want to be an artist?" I offer, and Ms. Walker chuckles again. But honestly, how can I figure out what I want to be when I'm still trying to sort out what I am?

I take the paper, my fingers brushing over the pencil drawings along the edge. A forest of charcoal trees, branching off across the page, idly drawn while my mind was elsewhere. But the innocent doodles take on a different meaning in today's light. My mind stretches back to my visions. Sharing a meal with a stranger, a tattoo climbing up his arm. An outstretched tree lined arm. Eerily similar to the smudged trees on this page.

"Alexandra, are you alright?" Ms. Walker puts a hand on my shoulder, and I jump. I wonder if she can see the rising panic in my eyes, mercury expanding, about to burst.

I handed in this paper last week. Before I started having my visions. Before I knew about this boy and his tattoo. My hands working from their own muscle memory, from something deep in my subconscious I wasn't aware of yet.

"Yeah, sure… I'm fine, everything is fine." But it's not. Everything is definitely not fine.

The P.A. system crackles to life, a grainy voice shouting through. "Ms. Walker, could you please send Alexandra to Mrs. Shaw's office immediately?"

"Yes, of course," Ms. Walker answers robotically. She fights to keep a neutral expression as she turns to me. "Alexandra, I suppose you better hurry to see your mother."

Dread crawled into my chest the moment I heard my name through the loudspeaker. Students filtered into class just in time to hear the announcement. They snicker and *oooh* and *ahhh* as if I were any other student being called out of class. But this isn't any other instance. My mom never associates with me at school. I'm not even sure what she does here, but I do know she'd never call me out of class and risk me falling behind.

Her office is located down a sterile hallway pretty much isolated from the rest of the school. I may as well be walking into the cave of a lion. Voices hiss louder the closer I get and when I turn the corner, there's Hannah outside the open office door, talking to my mom.

They both stop when I come into view.

"What's going on?" I ask. Hannah's face is tight. She's not going to cry, though, like someone in her situation might. She's furious and is trying not to show it. "Hannah, are you ok?"

"Hannah's fine," My mom answers instead. "She's just on her way back to class. Aren't you Hannah?" It's more of an order than a question and Hannah nods, obviously not trusting herself to speak. I stop myself from reaching out to grab her as she leaves and instead, follow my mom back into her office.

As I close the door, I see her name plaque in tarnished gold on the front. "Disciplinary Officer" it says underneath, and suddenly all of her previous comments and concerns fall in line. No wonder she was familiar with Kyle Larson's *before*. She probably has tabs on all the students here. I was so wrapped up with my friends and schoolwork to ever realize her role.

"Have a seat, Alexandra," she motions to the empty chairs on the opposite side of her desk. It's a big mahogany thing with a computer and one of those giant phones with lots of buttons that offices use. There isn't a single personal item in the entire space, definitely no picture of me, which I'm thankful for. The last thing

I need is some delinquent kid who may not know I'm her daughter seeing my picture and finding a new target.

"Is something wrong?" I ask, thinking about Hannah's expression. "Is Hannah ok?"

"Hannah is fine. That's not why I called you here. I wanted to apologize to you. About the way we left things last night." That is the last thing I expected her to say.

"You pulled me out of class to apologize?" My voice pitches high, betraying my surprise.

"I did. I feel terrible about how we are interacting lately. Being short with each other. I feel like you are slipping away from me. You don't have much longer before you graduate, and I don't want this time together to be dragged down with silly fights." She's being unusually kind. Despite knowing better, hope bubbles in my throat.

"I don't want to fight either. I don't know what is going on. I just feel so… weird. I don't know what's happening." I confess. I want to tell her more, the whole truth of what I've been experiencing, but something stops me.

"I think I've put too much pressure on you to prove yourself. You are working so hard, and you are doing so well here, but I realize I am being unfair to you. That you need time to be a kid, too."

She reaches across the desk for my hand. I hesitantly place it in her open palm, and she wraps her fingers around mine and squeezes. A supportive, motherly gesture. She hasn't touched me in a long time. We've never been much of a hugging family. Our acts of endearment are to clean the house or bring home dinner, so I don't know what to make of this.

"So, how *is* school going?" She asks, letting go of my hand and leaning back in her chair. Arms crossed; head tilted.

The mood shifts, a dark cloud appearing out of nowhere. I shudder, even though the room is stuffy and warm. So much for that apology.

"Same as always," I shrug, trying to be nonchalant and ignore the banging in my chest.

"You've been having a few outbursts in class lately. I just want to make sure there is nothing more going on with you?" Her words cast a net, hoping to catch me off guard. She may as well tilt her desk lamp right in my face. This is an interrogation, after all.

Stupid, stupid, stupid.

"I know. It's not like me. People have just been getting under my skin more than usual."

"Maybe I'll call Dr. Dave, set up a little check-in," she says, even though I haven't had to see Dr. Dave in weeks. It's more a threat than suggestion, which does nothing to ease my roiling stomach.

"No, no, it's cool. I just need to clear my head. It won't happen again." I promise. I do not want to go back to Dr. Dave and his moth-eaten sweaters and ear hairs.

"I sure hope not. Imagine how I feel, having my boss continually inform me of my daughter's behavior? It's embarrassing, Alexandra." Her lips curve up with a disapproving smile, the corners a sharpened knife cutting. I get smaller and smaller the wider it stretches.

"I'm sorry. Truly. I'll try harder to follow Kayla and Hannah's lead." I don't miss the way my mom stiffens at the mention of my friends. They're clearly not the role models she had in mind.

"You know, you could even spend a little less time with your friends and more time bringing your grades up." She tosses the grenade, waiting for my reaction. I play right into her hand because I'm a little stunned. My grades aren't perfect, but I mean, they aren't bad. And I'm trying. All I do is try. She hasn't mentioned anything about this before.

Something between us has shifted again.

"This is nice, Alexandra. I feel like we never have time to chat anymore. I'm going to miss it when you go away to school. Have you given any thought to where you'd like to go? Maybe you want to take a gap year and figure it out? There's no need to rush into anything." It's a light and airy question, but the way she says it makes the sentiment heavier.

We haven't talked a lot about my plans when I graduate from the Academy next year. It's a conversation she always tries to avoid. She wants me to live up to my potential, to be something great. But anytime I try to discuss the options for my future, she seems to shut me out. To hear her bring it up now seems out of character.

"I... have no idea," I shrug because it's true. I haven't looked at schools. I haven't even decided what I want to do. Hannah wants to study the books she's always reading, but that isn't right for me. Kayla wants to be an influencer, and Ms. Walker convinced her to consider Public Relations. But my future is still a swirl of gray clouds, nothing taking form.

"You should do something meaningful with your studies, be something more valuable to the community. A teacher, maybe. When you have your teaching degree, I'm sure I could pull some strings with the Academy to get you a position there."

My throat tightens. Working for the Academy. A future that leads me right back here, to this little town, to this insignificant life. Is that what I want for myself? I've always assumed I would be more than here, more than this, even if I don't entirely know what that means.

Why haven't I given this more thought?

"You're such a disappointment." Her judging eyes are a spider climbing up me. Her words trip me up.

"I'm what?" I ask, my breath clinging to my throat.

"I said I have another appointment. You have to go." She looks at me expectantly, but my stomach clenches again.

A taste more familiar than bile settles deep inside of me. I know, more than anything else, that I need to get out of this place.

# EIGHT

**CODING CLASS IS AS** disruptive as ever. And not just because of that conversation with my mom.

I'm doing all I can to focus on my task at hand, but Kyle Larson is carrying on in his usual fashion. Berating the students around him, causing a scene. He's zeroed in on Scott, again. A vulture, circling. Waiting for the right moment to descend.

"Scott… Hey Scott.…" He taunts, his voice echoing through the otherwise silent room. Mr. Morrison is just as good at ignoring Kyle's disruption as the rest of the class. All too afraid to pull his attention away, happy to let Scott take the fall. Better him than us, right? "Scott the Space Savior. That's what you call yourself right? In your fan fiction? It has a nice ring to it, all the S-words."

Scott tries to ignore him, doesn't look away from his screen, but his shoulders tense and his ears perk up. He's bracing for the coming blow, preparing for the worst.

And we all sit there holding our breath.

"I have some more for you—how about Scott the Socially Inept! Scott the Sterile!" This draws a few snickers from around the room, and Scott sinks down lower in his chair. "Scott the Psychotic!" Kyle's proud of that one.

"Psychotic starts with a 'p,' you idiot." It's out of my mouth before I even realize it. Every head turns to me and my heart skips. I don't know where it came from, I'm usually the one to run from danger, not poke it directly in its ego. But I have no patience for Kyle anymore. I have no patience for much today. Electricity runs through me. I'm untouchable.

"It sounds the same, *idiot.*" He mimics as that evil glint in his eye returns. Gears grinding. "What about you... Alexandra... Alexandra..." Again, he's making a big show, and everyone is watching him watch me. "Alexandra likes it in the a—"

"Mr. Larson. Do we have to have this same conversation again? Take your seat. Shut your mouth. And leave poor Miss Shaw alone."

Poor Miss Shaw. That will do me no favors. While I appreciate Mr. Morrison doing his actual job, bringing attention to Kyle will only fuel his fire. And now, that fire is pointed at me.

I had the balls to speak up. I don't know where it came from. I don't even know why. I owe Scott nothing. I just want to get through the day. But I couldn't contain the words, the anger, the pressure to just sit back and pretend everything is ok.

Kyle shoots me a snarl and I do my best to ignore him the rest of the class, but I can feel him staring at me. Seething.

When the bell rings, I'm already packed up and take off into the hallway. I need to put as much space as I can between me and him. Thank the creator he isn't the type of guy to have any interest in Yearbook class.

I plop into my desk, behind the computer monitor in the back corner. It's supposed to be an easy class, something that requires little focus or effort. Though there are a few overachievers in class who give the rest of us a bad name. Well, one overachiever anyway. Kimberly Marshall.

She nearly skips into the room, her giant camera slung around her neck, ponytail waving in the air, taunting me. I have no beef with Kimberly, but I guess Kayla's been rubbing off on me. Just looking at her today is enough to make me want to take a pair of scissors and cut that stupid ponytail right off.

I shake my head. It's cloudy and unfocused. Me, much the same.

I don't know what's going on with me, where all this anger and annoyance is coming from. But these visions... they're throwing me off. How can I just sit idly by when I may as well be losing my damn mind?

Maybe I should go see Dr. Dave. This has to be because of the accident. Because of the trauma. But that wouldn't explain away how real it all feels. How I know that I know that boy, even if I don't remember him.

And if I don't remember him, what else can't I remember? These are the kind of thoughts that will keep you up at night.

The kind of thoughts that make you want your mother... but

my mother has had an invisible wall around her lately. Whispering shitty comments under her breath, making me wonder if I'm hearing things. And then apologizing, making me wonder who that woman was and what she did with my real mother.

Our art teacher has taken her seat behind the front desk, content on leafing through a book than leading the class. It's Kimberly who is up at the front instead, barking out instructions and sharing her vision for the book. If only those were the visions I was struggling with.

I dump my messenger bag onto the empty chair beside me, searching for my phone. Items fall out of all the various pockets: lip balm, lint, a tampon with a ripped wrapper, spare change. Who even carries change with them anymore? My phone tumbles out and as I grab it, I notice what's underneath it.

A black guitar pick, with a stark white logo of a record store on the front. I recognize it, but I have absolutely no musical talent, or interest in music, so it definitely doesn't belong with my stuff. Story of my life these days. I pick it up and flip it over, revealing a silver heart drawn on it in sharpie. I knew it'd be there, somehow. I hold the pick, twirl it between my fingers until, just as before, I'm transported to somewhere that I don't belong, either.

*The music is loud, the crowd stifling. I'm surrounded by strangers, though it's one of the only times in my life when I don't feel entirely alone.*

*The energy in the room shifts, attention moving to the stage as the one local band most likely to make something of themselves appears. That's when I see him. Guitar pressed up against his chest. Fitted band shirt under button down flannel. Knee jumping in anticipation, like my heart.*

*The crowd parts as I move towards him. But when the guitars play a recognizable riff, they go wild. Jumping. Pushing. Screaming. I'm tossed around like a rag doll, but I never lose sight of him. Our eyes lock, and it's as if they're held there the entire show.*

*When the last chord is struck, the band takes a bow, heading for the exit. I should leave, but I can't. And apparently neither can he, until one of his bandmates grabs him by the arm and drags him stage left. Before he disappears completely, he flicks something towards me. I jump as the small piece of plastic hits my chest.*

My breaths are quick as I fall back into myself, back in Yearbook class, the intensity of the memory throwing me backwards into my chair. There's a sharp ringing in my ears from the loud music, even though it wasn't real. The same boy, the same tattoo. The same draw to him that I felt before.

I'm buzzing with adrenaline, both from the memory and the plan forming in my head. He's in a band. This is the first lead I've had. All I have to do is find what concerts are happening in the area and trace the connections through social media.

I log into the computer in front of me and hit up Google. There'd be nothing close to here; Clifton Hills is small. Like, really small. There's no music scene. Though some of the cities an hour away have shows, and it's not too hard to get to them if you know the right people.

None of my friends are those people, but Andy certainly is. Kayla says he was always trying to drag her to dive bars in the city to check out bands. She used to mock him, saying he only wanted to see them so he could claim he had saw them before they were cool. It was one of the reasons they broke up, apparently.

Google is failing me. Much like it did the other day when I was searching for that book. It seems less of a coincidence now than an omen. I can't dwell on that though, not when I'm steps away from breaking through this mystery, I know it.

I pick up my phone again and flip to Instagram to scroll through Andy's feed in search of anything having to do with a concert. He's definitely the type to humblebrag about the shows he's going to.

The same pictures that Kayla showed me stare back at me. The golden god, tossing a football. Leaning against a tree with a lazy, lopsided smirk. Intermixed with a group of his friends, wrestling around in their university's courtyard.

But that photo stops me mid-scroll. There are at least five bodies in the frame, limbs all strewn together in a human pretzel as they play-fight. It must be summer; they are all wearing short sleeves. I recognize a few of the other boys from the last time Andy visited, but there's one figure I can't seem to draw my eyes from.

His face is half out of frame and half-blocked by someone

else's head, but that isn't what catches my attention. I trail his arm down through the web of limbs to an elaborately inked tree line wrapping around his wrist and climbing up to just below his elbow. It's beautiful, breathtaking, but so eerily familiar. My stomach dips.

There's a lump in my throat and something tugging in my mind. It's the same tree line I've been seeing in my visions. The same person. And if he's wrestling with Andy in this photo, he's not just a figment in my head; something my brain is distracting me with. He's real and he's friends with Andy.

Which means maybe he'll be at Brian's party Friday night.

↑↑↑↑

"Kayla!" I call down the hall, trying to catch my friends as they head towards their lockers.

Kayla has the courtesy to look up from her phone. She stops to lean against the doorframe, blocking the way for the other students who are trying to get past.

"The party Friday? Count me in," I say enthusiastically.

"Well, it's about damn time," she responds, shoving her phone in her bag and linking her arm through mine. "I'm thrilled you finally came around. You won't regret it!"

"What changed?" Hannah asks, linking her arm through my other one, the two of them leading me down the hallway towards our next class.

"Does it matter? She's coming, that's what's important." Kayla says, flipping her hair over her shoulder and smiling at me.

Hannah doesn't say anything more, but she keeps looking at me out of the corner of her eye. I have the feeling she already knows what's changed.

# NINE

**EVERYTHING HAS STARTED TO** blur together. The flashes of memories mixing in with my reality and I have no idea what class I have next. Dread pools in my stomach when I realize my feet are leading me to biology.

Another class I share with Kyle Larson. There's no way he's going to forget about what happened this morning.

I sneak into the science lab quietly, hoping to go unnoticed. The room is only so big and of course, Kyle is at my heels as soon as I enter. I try to ignore him, take my place at my workstation, but he's standing too close to me. My body braces of its own volition. It's expecting him to do something cruel, but he just stands there, towering over me in a menacing way.

There's a putrid tinge to the air. Students around me are sniffing the air, their noses waving in every direction. I'm tempted aim my nose at Kyle, but that will probably just piss him off more.

"Alright, take your seats. Today is the day most of you have been waiting for." Mr. Jacobs's voice radiates through the lab and students immediately follow his command.

To my horror, Kyle sits down on the stool right beside me. He's so close, his leg brushing up against mine. It's a threat. A reminder that he's there. Out of my peripheral, he's staring at me, but I refuse to look at him and keep focused straight ahead. But my heart is racing, and I can't wait for this class to be over so I can run to the comfort and protection of my friends.

Mr. Jacobs walks to the side of the classroom and pulls a cart from the corner that I hadn't noticed. The cart is, undoubtedly, the source of the smell. As soon as it starts moving, noses crinkle as the odor wafts further around the room.

"Today, we will study the organ system of a complex organism. Today, we will be dissecting frogs." Mr. Jacobs picks up a scalpel and waves it through the air in a Z pattern. The class erupts into a mixture of groans and cheers.

Surprisingly, Kyle goes still beside me. He looks a little pale and visibly swallows.

There's a shift in the air.

"Don't tell me the all mighty Kyle Larson is afraid of a little frog dissection?" I whisper, though my voice intentionally cuts through the space between us. See how he likes it now that our roles are reversed.

"Shaw—" he starts, and his voice is a little rough with the unfamiliarity of saying my name. I slowly turn to face him, to take in his features for the first time since I've met him. Usually, I'm so busy avoiding his stare, but today, I'm not scared of him. His bleached-blonde hair is shaved short on the sides, but the longer hair atop his head is slicked back with gel.

His sharp eyes always seem to hold anger and hatred, but up closer, I can see that is masking something much deeper. Sadness. Loss. Loneliness.

I know those feelings well, or at least I did when I knew no one here. If it hadn't been for Kayla, maybe I would have turned out just like Kyle, isolated and alone, lashing out to protect myself. Okay, well, maybe not *exactly* like Kyle. But this realization makes my heart clench.

Suddenly I'm not so interested in giving him a taste of his own medicine.

Mr. Jacobs is slowly wheeling the cart from station to station, placing a silver tray in front of each pair of students. One of the wheels on the cart needs oiling and it squeaks a menacing squeak the closer it gets. Taunting us. He approaches our workstation and places a tray in front of us. There's a small cloth covering what I assume is the frog. Sharp, shiny medical utensils line the tray. Kyle stares at them blankly, his shoulders rigid.

With a hiss, a television screen comes to life at the front of the class. A young boy with dark hair and white lab coat graces the screen. There is no sound, but his actions mimic those of our teacher as he instructs us to remove the cloth covering the frog and pick up a scalpel.

Kyle reaches toward the tray, but I don't miss the tremor in his hand. He takes a deep breath, focusing all his energy into the one simple task. I stare at him, my mouth slightly open, waiting for what he's going to do. He's clearly struggling, something swirling inside of him, and I can't help but watch, waiting to see if this bully is going to implode. My fascination sickens me, but I can't look away.

His hand hovers over the scalpel. He's almost there. But then he jerks his arm back, cradling it across his chest as if he's hugging himself.

"I can't… I don't…" The words spill out through trembling lips.

It would be the perfect time to mock him. I have no doubt that he would take advantage of this vulnerability in any other person. But seeing Kyle Larson emotional—being an actual human being—I can't help but soften.

I lean closer, putting my hand on his back. "Are you ok—"

Kyle stands abruptly, his stool scraping against the floor with a horrible shriek. Everyone looks at him, surprised, as he darts across the room and stumbles out into the hall.

Mr. Jacobs stares curiously but doesn't move. With a huff, I gather my things and follow him, but not before sending our useless teacher a pointed glare.

"Hey Kyle, wait up!" I call, following him down the hall. He's going at a fast clip, and I jog to get within talking distance. "Hey, are you okay?"

He whirls on me, and I expect him to lash out, but there's sweat collecting on his forehead, his eyes are wide and full of terror. His chest is heaving. He can't catch his breath. He's a cornered animal staring at me. Wild eyes. Teeth bared. Hackles up. I put my hands up to show I mean no harm.

"I think you're having a panic attack. It's ok. Sit down, put your head between your legs, and take some deep breaths." I motion to the floor in front of a bank of lockers, repeating the steps Dr. Dave has told me many times. I'm sure he'd feel more comfortable in private, but I'm not even sure I could get him to follow me anywhere.

He does as I instruct and sinks to the floor, his legs bent so that he can bury himself between his knees. I count aloud with him.

"Deep breath… one, two three… and now let it out… one, two, three…" His chest heaves in and then out, slowly starting to calm into a more comfortable pattern.

After a few more minutes, he finally raises his head and stares directly across the hall, pretending I'm not even there. His eyes are rimmed red and there's a blush streaking across his neck. He's embarrassed. I have the upper hand for once.

"What happened back there?" I ask gently. I fully expect him to scowl at me and take off, but he stays seated next to me, seeming to collect his thoughts.

"I don't know. One minute, I was planning how to make you pay for what you did to me in the computer lab." He glances at me sideways, a look of pure disdain. "And the next, all I could see was that scalpel. I… well you wouldn't believe me if I told you." He mumbles, running his hand through his hair.

"Try me," I say, remembering saying those same words to

Hannah earlier this week and how good it felt to confide in her.

"I felt like… I had been here before? Not here, here. But holding a blade. I saw myself…" He trails off with a grimace, the words too hard to speak aloud. I put a reassuring hand on his arm, expecting him to flinch, but he doesn't.

Instead, he places his hand not far from mine and pushes up his long sleeves. As the fabric bunches, I see skin. Skin with faint lines around the inside of his wrist. They're small and white, and it takes me a minute to realize they're scars.

"I've had these scars for as long as I can remember, but I can't remember where they came from. I've asked my parents, but they always give me the same lame story about a thorn bush. I remember that thorn bush. But the story always felt a little wrong to me. And then as soon as I saw that scalpel, I had this urge to… man, I can't even tell you." He lowers his head down between his knees again.

"It's okay. You don't need to tell me." I say. A weird feeling comes over me and I realize it's a feeling of connection. I'm having a very intimate and intense conversation with Kyle Larson. I want to pinch myself to see if this is even real.

Silence fills the hallway. My thoughts are spiraling. Kyle's urge feels very similar to the visions I've been having of things that feel like they happened that I don't remember. His story of his past with the thorn bush not feeling right is the same as how I've been starting to feel about my own past. If this is happening to Kyle, too, then maybe I'm not going crazy. Maybe what is happening to me is really, actually happening to me.

I shake my head, trying to clear my thoughts. Not knowing what to do next.

"Why are you so mean?" I blurt out, unsure where that thought came from. It's a genuine question, though.

My words seem to confuse him. He furrows his brow, not sure how to respond. His eyes dart around the hallway as if he's searching for someone, not sure what to do with himself. I say nothing but wait for him to continue.

When he finally does, "I don't want to be" is what he chooses to say. It makes me smirk.

"Maybe you don't want to be, but you are, Kyle. You pick on everyone. The first time you saw me, you pushed me into my locker. You humiliated me in front of our class and mocked my dead father," I challenge, and he has the courtesy of cringing at his former actions.

"I'm sorry." It's a whisper offered as a white flag. "I don't want to be mean; I just don't know how else to be. There's just all this… pain. Don't you feel it too?"

I'm about to say no, definitely not. But I consider him. I consider this last year. I consider the accident and my mother and father. And there is pain. Maybe not in the same way he's describing, but I know what he means.

"Even so, inflicting pain on other people to relieve your own, that's not cool. You know that, right?" I'm standing a ground I've never dared to make before. People don't confront Kyle Larson. People don't even talk to him. I don't know where this is coming from, but he seems less of a bully and more a scared child, lost and a little lonely.

He's going over something in his head, his mouth flopping open. It takes him a while to sort out his words. "I know. I don't think that's naturally me. I mean, coming here, well, it's supposed to *reform* us, right? Make us live up to our true potential? But I have felt less and less like myself the minute I walked through those doors. Like I'm losing who I am, not finding it. Do you know how that feels?" He pulls away from me, the vulnerability in his words creating more space between us.

But I lean closer, those words drawing me in because they match the feeling I've had myself.

"This place, they try to make us better. But what does that really mean?" he asks, and I don't know how to answer. "Who decides what is better? We make choices, and those choices dictate our future. We change depending on our experiences and everything we do is an active decision that makes up who we are. That's what you said." Kyle lets my Nature vs Nurture speech hang between us. Who we are told to be versus who we are.

"So, then decide to be better. Not their version of better, but your own." I respond, brushing my hands on my knees before standing up. "Would you like to join us for lunch?" When I ask, his initial reaction is the Kyle scowl, but it quickly softens, and I realize how much he wants to join us for lunch. But instead of accepting, he shakes his head.

"Thank you, but I think I need some time to myself."

He stands too and takes off down the hallway without giving me a second glance.

# TEN

**KAYLA AND HANNAH ARE** already at our table when I enter the cafeteria. The chorus of soda cans hissing open creates a hum in the background, the usual olive oil, and dirt smell infiltrating my nostrils. I'm sick to my stomach. The idea of grabbing something from the meal plan menu is as unappealing as the meal plan itself.

I head straight for our table, but a cloud of whispers surrounds me. People look up from their lunch trays in unison as I pass. It reminds me of a scene from a movie where all heads turn at once, and I'd be amused if it wasn't so friggin' creepy. The hairs stand up on my neck, my arms prickling with goosebumps.

Everyone is staring at me.

When I reach our table, the spell is broken and everyone goes back to their own business. I look at my friends, to see if they notice, but they're focused on the food in front of them. Kayla picks idly at a limp green-brown salad from the cafeteria. Hannah has started brown bagging her lunch like Ms. Walker, but it's unopened in front of her. She says it's healthier to know exactly what we're eating and tried to get us to start making lunches too. But I worry that this isn't about being healthy, but her trying to control how much she eats.

She has been so withdrawn today, acting a little quieter and more contemplative than usual. How do you know if your friend is in trouble? Is it when other students start staring at them that you finally start to pay attention? Though no one seems to have noticed everyone staring at me.

"Are people… are people staring at me?" I whisper, running my eyes across the room, heads turning any time I land on them. After this morning and the scene I caused, I can't be surprised. Word travels so damn fast in this place.

But it's my mother I worry about. She heard about what happened in English class, she'll no doubt hear about my Kyle run-ins. One more thing I will have done to embarrass her. I can't wait for that conversation.

"They aren't staring at you Alexandra; they're staring at me. They're always staring at me," Kayla's confidence is twofold today, and I don't have the patience to deal with it. Once again, she barely looks up from her phone.

"No, really. I feel like everyone is watching me. Are they saying anything, Kayla? You always know what is going on." I try again and Kayla does me the courtesy of putting her phone down on the table to look at me.

"The gossip mill is closed today. I have nothing to report. Unless you want to talk to me about Brian's party tonight, I am right out of information."

Brian's party. Right. The chance to maybe put a face to the boy I keep seeing. To finally get some answers about what exactly is going on with me.

"So, I'll come 'round yours at seven? We can primp and have a couple drinks and then head over to Brian's?" Kayla says it more as a command, but sneaking drinks into my home, past my mother, makes my stomach turn.

That's what normal seventeen-year-olds do, don't they? They sneak beers and joints and go to parties on Friday nights to blow off steam. But there's a swirling in my belly, a pit in my gut telling me it's a bad idea.

"Why don't I come to the dorm? It's on the way to Brian's, it makes more sense for me to come to you," I offer instead and her face splits into a huge, toothy smile, the kind of smile that rewards you for saying the right thing.

"Make sure you wear something..." Kayla trails off as she gives me a once over. She studies the fading pink lace tank top peeking out from under my school issued blouse, my loose-fitting trousers. I stopped wearing the plaid skirt with knee-highs, the uniform option girls here mostly favor, and Kayla has noticed.

I'm a mix of a before and after segment on a TV show. Clearly, with no idea of what my style is anymore. I glance down at my frumpy, comfortable outfit, not sure what to do with myself. "I won't let you down, I promise."

Satisfaction shadows her face as she leans across to kiss me on the cheek. "So tonight then. I promise you won't regret it!" She flips her hair over her shoulder, eyes sparkling victoriously.

Regret. I don't know what answers wait for me at this party. What is going to be revealed to me if the boy I keep seeing appears? Maybe it's not a great idea after all. Shaking things up. I could just keep pretending nothing is going on. Just make it to the end of graduation so I can get out of this place, as was always my plan. I can't shake the lingering dread. I try to push it aside as I slump into my seat.

Hannah hasn't said anything, but she's studying me over the top of the book she's reading as if she can hear my thoughts. She closes the book and meets my eye. I smile weakly, reach out, and tilt the book up so I can see the cover. She's reading the book she loaned me that I didn't read—*Never Let Me Go* by Kazuo Ishiguro. But it's a different copy, a different cover. The one my mother confiscated clearly didn't make it back to her, as she said it would.

"What's it about?" I ask her to distract myself from my thoughts.

"It's about a group of kids at a boarding school, who have been cut off from society. They live their days at the school, not realizing the full truth of what is actually happening there." Her eyes narrow as she says this.

"Well, what is actually happening there?" Kayla jumps in, annoyed that she left out the best part.

"I can't spoil it; everyone has to figure that out for

themselves. When they read the book, I mean," she says, sending Kayla back into a slouch.

Headmaster Johnson marches into the cafeteria, and the temperature drops a few degrees. The chatter grows quieter, everyone's eyes on their own lunches. Hannah quickly shoves her book into her bag.

The headmaster approaches Ms. Walker at her usual table and they exchange a few words, too quiet for me to make out. Ms. Walker's expression fights to remain neutral, but there's a small tick of her lips. Once the Headmaster is gone, the noise returns along with my thoughts.

"I don't know if Ms. Walker is going to be here much longer. Headmaster Johnson seems like he has it out for her," I say, and Hannah's head whips around to the front of the cafeteria where Ms. Walker is left sitting, staring out at all the students with a dazed expression.

"I hope not. She's one of the only teachers who isn't a completely extra," Kayla mutters, spearing a cherry tomato with her fork.

"Doesn't this place ever seem weird to you? Like, it belongs in one of your books, Hannah. A bunch of so-called troubled students thrown together, isolated from society? Living life like there is nothing outside the school walls?" I gesture around us, at everyone minding their own business, completely oblivious to anything else that could be out there.

"And then all the rumors? About the tunnels under the school. About the students disappearing. Going wild."

"What are you getting at?" Kayla asks, somewhat annoyed.

An ear-piercing wail echoes through the cafeteria, answering for me. The entire room goes quiet, the sound ringing through the air. Students start to shuffle and glance around, trying to figure out where it's coming from. Then it sounds again, from another direction, and everyone's heads whip towards the wall of windows that peer out towards the cliffs.

There's a figure out there, in the school's yard. At first, I don't recognize him. His bleached-blond hair is wild, a mess atop his head, falling into his face as he runs. Eyes wide, desperate.

"What's Kyle doing? I was just talking to him…" I'm not sure if I say this out loud, my words caught along with everyone's attention.

The cafeteria fills with whispers, bodies moving closer to the windows. I catch some of what they're saying, though I want to pretend I don't hear them. He runs frantically across the property towards the edge of the cliff, a guttural wail escaping from his wide, wicked smile.

Headmaster Johnson is outside, along with two security guards. They chase him, but he keeps darting out of reach. His limbs flail wildly. They have nothing to grab hold of, to reel in.

My heart is in my throat as I watch him edge closer and closer to the cliff. We all watch, holding our breath, as the guards gain on him. One cracks a baton against Kyle's knee. He crumbles to the ground, another shattering cry, but this one is full of a different type of pain. He is laying in a heap, still, the guards and Headmaster surrounding him to block our view. They fumble with a syringe, and press it into his bare arm.

One guard leans down, linking his arms under Kyle's, hoisting him up from the ground. The other guard dutifully grabs his legs, and they slowly walk his limp body back towards the door behind the school.

Headmaster Johnson lingers at the edge of the cliff for a moment longer, running his hand through his graying hair. He's too far to see clearly, but there are wrinkles on his forehead. He's annoyed, more frustrated than worried. He stares out at the rough water in contemplation, picking a stray piece of something off his suit, before turning and wandering back.

Slowly, all the students turn from the window and return to their tables, the noise level barely above a whisper. We've all heard the rumors, the stories, but we've never witnessed it before.

Kyle Larson has gone wild.

# ELEVEN

**THE SCHOOL DAY IS** cut short, and we're sent home early. I walk with Kayla and Hannah toward the dorms until I have to break off to head to my house. But I don't want to leave them. I don't want to be alone without their company, their reassurance.

"Do you think he'll be okay?" I ask, breaking our silence. Kayla shrugs, fiddling with her hair while she leans up against the street sign at the fork in the road. She's hardly said two words since we left school, highly sus for Kayla.

"He'll be fine. He didn't jump. That's the important part," Hannah answers, her words a little harder than her usual tone. She seems on edge. A little annoyed.

"Are you okay?" I ask, and she bristles.

"I'm fine." Hannah isn't one for many words, but her answer is clipped, even for her.

"You good Kayla?" I turn my attention back to her. She's still tugging on her hair, wrapping it around her fingers until the circulation cuts off. It's subtle, her movements graceful, but I know these anxious habits enough to know she's shook.

"Yeah, just fab. Hey, how about we blow off some steam? Hit the mall, find something to wear to the party tonight?"

I can't believe anyone can think about a party after what we just witnessed, let alone going shopping. That just goes to show what kind of place this is. People put their heads down; keep moving forward as if nothing has happened.

I can't just let go of what happened. But I can't let Kayla down, either. I've been so irritated with her lately; this should smooth things over. Not to mention, going to the party is my chance to find out more about what is going on here. For my and Kyle's sake.

"Definitely." I give her a tight smile, allowing her to lead Hannah and me towards the very small strip mall down the road from the Academy.

⇈⇈

"Alexandra, what in the bloody hell are you doing in there?" Kayla's voice shrills through the change room door. My uniform slacks are still around my ankles, and I'm staring at myself in the mirror.

Same pale skin, same chaotic red hair. Pink polka-dot underwear and matching bra. This is how I've always looked, but I don't recognize myself. The outfits Kayla picked out are strewn in little balls at my feet. They're all soft, pale colors that belong in my closet, but they aren't right when I hold them up against me.

"Don't you think these colors make me look like an Easter egg?" I ask, kicking at the dresses with my flats. "What happened to the dresses Hannah picked out for me?"

"They're all black, Alexandra. Since when is that your style?" she calls back. I don't need to see her to know that she's rolled her eyes and Hannah's shrunk away.

But I get it. It's not my style. I'm not trying to be a pain in the ass, but I don't want to show up to this party looking like My Little Pony wearing a doily. I feel ridiculous.

"It just... doesn't seem right. It doesn't feel like that's me. That it was ever me." My closet is a rainbow, but I'm a brewing storm and nothing feels... right.

Kayla doesn't say anything else, and I picture her stalking through the store, slowly placing piece after piece from my selected wardrobe back on the shelves. The wrong shelves, probably, which she knows drives me absolutely mental.

I hold up one of the dresses again, trying to think of the last time I was dressing for a party. I've never been much for parties. Before we moved, I certainly wasn't invited to many, but that never bothered me. I didn't even go to junior prom, though we weren't the type to go to prom anyway.

*In fact, we were going to throw an anti-prom, just the two of us. Dressed down in our least fancy outfits, eating junk food, and listening to music that didn't suck. I wore my favorite pair of worn in jeans, him in one of his band shirts. The one that fit him just right, clinging to his strong arms, accenting the shadows of his tree tattoo.*

The dress drops to the floor, pooling at my feet. The overhead lights are suddenly too bright, and I strain against them, seeing spots. It happened again. Another weird vision, taking me somewhere else completely. That stranger, again. So close I could smell him, a woodsy scent that was intoxicating, but also calming

My heart pounds. My body has caught fire, too warm after battling my insecurities and discomfort stemming from studying myself in the change room mirror. The walls of the stall start to close in on me, the air thick, getting stuck in my throat. All my thoughts press down on me, stopping me from caring about a stupid shopping trip.

I pull up my slacks and stick my head out of the stall. Kayla and Hannah are gone. I scan the store and can't see them anywhere. I book it to the front door, desperate to be anywhere but here.

The chill in the air is a relief to my burning skin. I can't go back into that store. The dank lighting, the perfectly dressed mannequins. Everything was screaming at me, pointing at me, mocking me.

Like I'm a phony.

And maybe I am. Whatever has been going on with me lately, nothing seems right. Nothing feels right. I don't even know who I am anymore.

"Alexandra, there you are." Kayla is suddenly beside me, like

I was the one who took off. "Come with me, you're going to love this." She grabs my sleeve, pulling me along the street. Hannah follows behind us, dragging her feet. She's more quiet than usual, clearly wanting to be anywhere but here.

The strip mall is quiet, a little run down. A few of the window fronts have boards over the glass and crooked, paint-chipped signs. It's been a while since I've been here, and it's only gotten more and more run down. I can't imagine anything Kayla could show me that I would "love."

She drags us a little further to the storefront at the end. It's a little accessory store, selling hair ties and makeup and costume jewelry. Kayla wears a huge smile as she pushes me through the door, blocking my way back out when I finally see what she is so excited about.

Glamor Makeovers.

It's a neon sign hanging in the back of the store above a makeup station and what seems to be a salon chair. It may as well be an electric chair.

"I'm not getting in that." I say, taking a few steps back towards the door.

"Oh, come on, it'll be fun! Perfect for the party tonight!" Kayla is so excited, smiling ear to ear, and even though every part of me wants to flee, I can't bring myself to disappoint her. This is supposed to be a distraction from what happened today.

"Ugh… ok fine. But I get to veto anything that makes me feel too much like a clown," I say, climbing up into the chair. Hannah's to my right, admiring all the nail polish options, but she won't meet my eyes in the mirror. She's not avoiding me, but she's certainly keeping herself at a distance.

A sales assistant approaches, looking entirely bored, so it doesn't take much for Kayla to convince them that she'll do the makeover.

I paw through the makeup set out on the counter in front of us as Kayla wrestles my long locks into some elaborate 'do. Now that I'm basically held down against my will, Kayla takes this opportunity to bring up one of her favorite topics: boys.

"Maybe you'll meet someone at the party tonight, Alexandra. There ought to be a large crowd." I'm not looking at her, but I can hear the smirk in her voice.

"Ha, yeah. Right. Maybe." My words are more sarcastic than I mean them. But the idea of meeting someone right now, when everything feels so uncertain and confusing, is the most ridiculous thing in the whole world.

"No really, you've been here for a while, it's about time you let your guard down. Maybe even kiss someone. There must be some boy who has caught your eye," Kayla says, matter of fact. To her, the idea that I haven't been interested in anyone is unfathomable.

"Or girl," Hannah adds shyly, concentrating on my nails, but her ears perk up; she's curious also.

"Alexandra isn't interested in girls, right Alexandra?" Kayla's eyes are wide as she meets mine in the mirror expectantly.

"I'm not interested in anyone," I answer, avoiding any confirmation of my sexuality. Kayla says it as if it's a big deal, but

I've always felt that attraction is attraction. Does it matter who it's to as long as they aren't assholes? "Everyone here is... boring. They're all the same, aren't they? None of them have done anything remotely interesting to make me interested. Present company excluded, obviously."

"Obviously," Kayla repeats smugly. There's a pause in the conversation, a short, awkward moment, before Kayla and Hannah continue primping and pulling at me. "Well, maybe one of Andy's mates will catch your fancy? A college boy, there, that's what you need."

"What I need?" I roll my eyes, my voice flat. "I don't need anything. Let alone anyone."

I play it cool, but my pulse immediately picks up because Kayla is right. One of Andy's mates is exactly what I'm looking for. And will help me get to the bottom of what is happening once and for all.

It has to be that easy, right? Seeing him tonight with Andy will remind me that I do know him, that I've seen him in passing or something. He's just hanging out in my subconscious, taking me on dates to Italian restaurants and other various daydream scenarios. That's got to be it, right?

Kayla sighs, putting the brush down. Hannah's reflection in the mirror wears a satisfied smile. "What?" I ask, suddenly embarrassed for zoning out, daydreaming again.

"Nothing. It's just—you look great." She smiles again and I realize why. I'm holding an eyeliner pencil, something I have no idea how to properly apply, and yet somehow, I've lined my eyes almost perfectly. Charcoal smudges, a distinctive cat-lick up the corner. It's a different look, but my hands drew it almost out of habit. Almost as if I've been doing this all my life.

I like the look of it—armor on my face as I prepare to step onto the battlefield of a high school party. Still the new student, still the girl who killed her father. At least my look is something I can change.

I look like myself, lined cat-eye and all, just a little more defined. Maybe even a little pretty. Until my image in the mirror blurs, the lights behind me, fading into dark. I'm no longer in the store, but a crowded venue.


*The show hasn't started yet, but the crowd is electric. Bodies press up against each other, the anticipation creating an intensity that can only exist in the minutes before a band hits the stage. It's one of my favorite moments, the only time I feel truly free.*

*My stormy-blue eyes scan the crowd. A thick cat's eye is elongated against my upper cheek. A ring of fire-red hair pulled back tight on one side, cascading in rippling waves on the other. That's when I see him.*


"You look good, but not *that* good," Kayla laughs, stepping in front of the mirror to obstruct my view of myself. I've been staring, zoned out. Somewhere else again, with someone else.

And by the end of tonight, I'll know who that someone is.

# TWELVE

**THE WALK HOME IS** somber. The street is quiet, and I'm almost convinced I'm the sole creature alone in a city after the apocalypse. I left Kayla and Hannah at their dorms, delighted with my new makeover and a plan to meet back up with them later for the party.

The afternoon was a good distraction, but now that I'm alone again, I keep hearing Kyle's bone-chilling wails in my head. Seeing his body slumped against the ground. All his control sucked out of him entirely.

I can't help but feel a little responsible. Me, standing up to him in computer lab. Then connecting with him, his confession about the memories that he had when he picked up the scalpel. I can't shake the thought that I somehow caused him to go wild. That something I said, or did, is what set him off.

And now…who even knows where he is. If he's ok. Was a

simple act of kindness enough to derail him and cause him to go wild? It doesn't make sense.

Our home, modest to all degrees with outdated wallpaper barely clinging to its bones, is as welcoming as it ever is. But my mother is sprawled on the couch, arm swept raggedly over her eyes. One leg stretched out across the fabric and the other bent at the knee, so her foot is planted on the floor. Her summer dress is pulled taut between the two.

I assumed she would have heard about what happened at school. Assumed she would be waiting for me with questions and concern. I did not expect to see her sprawled on the couch mid-day like a hungover college kid skipping class. Did she even go to work at all?

I try "Mom?" but she doesn't stir. A mess of paperwork with the Academy's logo at the top litters the coffee table. Her cell phone is a corpse drowned in a sticky ring left by a glass that is no longer in sight. The light on her phone is flashing urgently, but she's in no shape to answer it.

Her breath staggers and there's a soft snore accompanying the rise and fall of her chest. The hypnotic movement of her breathing draws me in until my vision blurs and the pressure builds behind my eyes again.

*My mother, her long hair suddenly short, the way she used to wear it when I was a child. I'm no longer looking down on her, but up at her from the floor. A much younger, shorter version of myself. There's a heaviness in my stomach, something akin to hunger and desperation, a longing that I haven't felt in years. A smell invades my nostrils, something sharp and musky, body odor mixed with garbage.*

As quickly as I was transported, I'm drawn back to the present. To my mother as I know her, asleep on the couch in front of me.

My visions have always been about the stranger. But this one of my mother but not my mother stirs something completely different inside of me. It's not the same electric excitement I've been feeling, but a deep and heavy dread. A knowing that's been suppressed.

I can't quite dig it out, and I know that a part of me doesn't want to. Because whatever I've buried this deeply can't be good.

I kick off my shoes and set my messenger bag down quietly by the front door before heading up the stairs to my mother's room. I couldn't bring myself to buy anything for the party. With a little luck, there might be something in her closet with a neckline that isn't stretched out. Maybe it will even meet Kayla's standards.

I'm elbow deep in her walk-in closet, so I don't hear her come in the room behind me. "What are you doing?" Her words are thick and heavy, but they slap me. I whip around, yanking a flimsy charcoal blouse with me. Her eyes dart between me and the contents of the closet. Her crossed arms a shield against her chest.

"Trying to find something to wear to a party tonight." My tone is even, but my mind is spinning with questions about her smudged makeup and slow movements. They're foreign to me, but the familiarity is suffocating, and it puts me on edge.

"I didn't know there was a party!" Her voice is unnaturally loud. Fake. She's obviously trying too hard to be cheerful, and it backfires, surprising us both. "I heard about what happened at school. Are you okay? That blouse won't do you any favors." She grabs it out of my hands and pushes me carefully from the closet as she flips through the hangers, eying her collection of clothing.

"Do you think a party is what you should be doing tonight?" She asks, her tone a warning.

"Mom, everyone's going. You said you wanted me to find my place at this school and try to fit in. How better to do that than to go?" I seem to have got her with that one.

"Are there going to be parents at this party?" she tries again. I'm pretty sure she's searching for an excuse to say no.

"Of course," I answer immediately even though I don't know if that's true. She deflates. I can't tell if it's relief or frustration.

"I don't know, Alexandra, the way you have been acting… you said yourself you are overtired. Don't you think it would be better if you stayed home to rest?"

"Mom, please. I need to go to this party," I say, but it's too urgent. She turns quickly from the closet, eyes narrowed.

"Here." She hands me a simple black shift dress and I hold it up to my body. It cuts just above the knee and has a high neckline with no sleeves. Presentable, but not presenting too much.

"Mom, it's perfect!" I say, reaching for the dress, but she pulls it out of my reach.

"What's on your face?" she asks as if it's the first time she's seen me since I've been home.

"Uh… it's just a bit of makeup. Kayla and Hannah gave me a makeover after school." I self-consciously bring my hands to my face, but I don't want to smear it. I freeze there in an awkward somewhat defensive stance.

"Wipe it off, you look ridiculous." She says simply. My heart falls into my stomach, the air suddenly heavy.

"It's just a little makeup Mom, no big deal."

"It is, in fact, a big deal. You are my daughter and what you do reflects back on me and my position with your school. Makeup is not part of your dress code."

"But this party isn't a school function," I retort, panic building. I can see where this conversation is going, and I need to do everything I can to avoid it.

My mom glares at me, scrunching her dress into a ball, and throwing it on the closet floor before closing the door.

"Are you okay?" She clearly isn't okay. The teenager in me wants to yell and stalk out of the room, but she's been acting so strange lately. A grenade, and I can never tell if I'm holding the pin. Most of the time she's stoic; a bottle holding the storm inside, so I never see what's brewing. But every so often, the cork pops with the pressure and I end up drenched.

"It's just a headache. Come on, I'll drive you to your party."

My stomach clenches. I just want to leave. "No, that's ok. I'm going with Kayla and Hannah. I said I'd meet them at their dorms."

"Well, I'll take you to the dorms then." It's no longer an offer, it's an order. I don't remind her that I haven't changed out of my school uniform. I take the olive branch and hold it close, not daring to say another word that might tip her back in the other direction.

The drive is long and quiet. It's going to storm; the clouds are getting darker. My head is leaning against the window, the vibrations from the engine a hypnotic rhythm. I let it lull me into a trance, and that's when it happens again.

*I'm staring out the car window at the darkening sky, waiting for the moment the rain falls. Trying to push down the feeling that keeps rising in my throat. I don't get carsick; this is something else. A taste that I've had to swallow down too many times before.*

*I'm supposed to be meeting someone and am trying to text them to let them know I'm running late. But my phone has no signal, each text is left unsent. I chuck it into my purse at my feet, but it lands on the floor instead.*

*"You know, Alexandra, I appreciate that you have found a friend in this boy, but I don't know how I feel about you spending time with someone who is older than you."*

*"He's just a boy, Mother. He's harmless."*

*"Harmless? Hardly. You're a dreamy distraction for a boy like that. He sees your big house. Your pretty features. And he must have it. Consume it. But that shimmer will wear off, the allure will fade, and then he will see you for what you really are."*

*"And what is that Mother? What am I really?" I pretend I don't care what she thinks, but there's a pit in my stomach*

*expecting what she will say, what she always says.*

*"Nothing. Alexandra, you are nothing. There is nothing special about you, you are just like every other girl, and he will come to see that, and he will leave you in pieces."*

The slam of the brakes rips me back to reality and I struggle to calm my racing heart. It takes a minute to realize that we're sitting outside of the dorm, that my mother is waiting for me to get out. Again, she doesn't say anything. She's angry, but I can't for the life of me figure out why.

It doesn't make sense, but nothing about today makes sense. Nothing about these last few weeks make sense. And now I'm having visions about my mother. My mother knowing this boy.

My mind is reeling, there is a pit in my stomach—a gurgle of worry. These flashes are starting to feel less and less like visions.

They're feeling more like memories.

# THIRTEEN

**I SHOW UP TO KAYLA'S** dorm, my hands empty and a stone in my gut. Kayla's a newly transformed butterfly fluttering around her room in the most exotic colors, putting me to shame. Hannah is in the little dorm kitchen, mixing vodka with some kind of red juice she pours it into three glasses. She hands us each a red cup and we raise our hands into the air, crashing the cups together so quickly that some liquid spills out.

"To us!" We giggle, licking the sticky sweet tonic from our fingers.

Kayla eyes my uniform. I'm about to plead the fifth, before I know it, she choreographs a movie makeover montage. Pulling out outfit after outfit form her overstuffed closet, demanding I twirl on command. All that's missing is a spunky pop number.

She settles on a black shift dress that rivals the one from my mother's closet. I change into it quickly while they chitchat in

Kayla's sitting area. When I open the bathroom door for my entrance, I swear I hear them gasp.

"You look incredible!" Hannah whispers, jumping up from the chair and rushing to my side. My heart fills. I may not know what is going on with me, but at least I'll look the part as I try to figure things out.

"I did pretty good, if I do say so myself," Kayla agrees, holding out her phone to take a picture for Instagram. She motions for us to gather closer. I let out a groan to make my annoyance known but allow her to herd me into that tiny square so she can present me to all her loyal followers.

Before I know it, we are on the stoop of Brian's house, our bellies full of liquid courage.

The bass of the music throbs through Brian's front door before we even open it, seeping through my skin and into my veins. Keeping time with my beating heart. I'm already floating, flushed from the drinks we downed too quickly.

The drumming beat gives me a strong awareness of my existence. My new existence. I wear a confidence I haven't worn in years, a sense of self that has been absent ever since we moved here. In the six months that I've been here, Brian has had many parties, but tonight feels different. I feel different.

"I'm going to get us drinks!" Kayla yells over the music as she beelines for the kitchen. Brian's house is a modest bungalow. It's surprisingly spacious, but with the number of bodies pressed together in the shadows of the dim lighting it's hard to tell.

Fairy lights twinkle across the ceiling. Crisscrossed limbs

sprawl atop the furniture. Bodies explore other bodies in the corners. Neon fliers coat the walls, making it more nightclub than living room. They scream out expressions:

Wake Up!
Remember Us!

Not-so-subtle catch phrases from our peppy student council announcing various school events. Brian must have pulled them from the bulletin boards and taped them up here instead.

The crowd is mostly students from the Academy; Kimberly Marshall, standing with her hands on her hips as if she's mid-debate and not at a party. Joe Walden, sitting in the middle of the couch with a book on his lap, tearing bits of green into little pieces on top of it. I don't see Andy and his friends. Other than a few nods, I float through the room almost invisibly. Which is what I prefer.

"Ladies! You came!" Brian rushes up to Hannah and me, a little too close for comfort. Out of his school uniform, he perfectly fills out the stoner stereotype with his oversized shorts and backwards ball cap.

"Wouldn't miss it for the world," I respond with little enthusiasm.

"I don't see Andy anywhere. You don't think he bailed on his own party, do you?" Kayla pushes Brian out of the way with the red cup she's holding out to me, her eyes still crawling over the room.

"There's a sunroom in the back of the house." I barely hear

Hannah over the music.

"You're brilliant." Kayla kisses her swiftly on the forehead, setting Hannah's neck aflame, and pulls her through the crowd towards the back of the house. I take another swig from the cup of beer, nearly empty already, and follow them closely.

Energy builds as we saunter through the house. An electric anticipation radiates off Kayla as she homes in on Andy's location. But I feel it too. I'm a live wire at the thought of putting a face to that forest tattoo. If I'm right and he's at this party, will I recognize him? Will he slide perfectly into this empty space that has consumed my life lately, the void full of questions and conflicting thoughts?

Voices carry from the back of the house where there are no other partygoers, just a long hallway, and a half-open door. Kayla pushes her way through it with the confidence of someone who belongs there.

"Gentlemen," she interrupts, glancing quickly around the room, pausing pointedly on Andy. A smile tugs slowly at his lips as he registers her. "I have arrived!"

I follow in the wake of her eye line. A handful of boys-turned-twenty-something-men hover around a pool table. Beers in hand, deep in conversation. I steady my breath, anxiety slowly releasing as I realize that I vaguely recognize them all from previous parties. There's no sign of the boy with the forest tattoo. A mix of relief and disappointment.

"Why Kayla, long time no see. You're as fit as ever. Come give us a closer look." One of Andy's friends holds out an arm, mocking her accent in a teasing tone. Hannah fades into the din of conversation. She's weirdly comfortable, a contradiction to her quietness. I hang back along the outer edge of the room at the far end of the pool table. Far less comfortable.

I have always been a little jealous of the way Kayla got on with the people around her. It comes so naturally to her. It is something I can never manage, something that always makes me feel a little out of place until it's just the three of us again.

My fingertips run across the green felt of the pool table as I mindlessly circle around it, putting more distance between me and the rest of them. Someone walks into the room, and my head snaps over to the outstretched arm passing a red cup to Andy. Of course, an inky forest wraps itself around the wrist.

Body freezes. Eyes jolt up. I'm locked in the piercing gaze of sharp gray clouds. Sweat slithers down my spine.

It's him.

I don't recognize him, but those piercing green-gray eyes hold a strange reminder of something. All of my senses tingle. The feel of his hand in mine. The music around us takes over. I'm transported again.

*Laying on a hardwood floor, surrounded by vinyl, the static of a record player in the background, music all around me. All around us. My head falls to the right. To a boy with ink-black trees curling up his forearm, which is thrown casually across his face to shade his eyes from everything. Everything but the music. Everything but me.*

My eyes snap open and the room feels three times smaller. He's looking at me, holding my stare. Every instinct I have tells me to break away, to run, but I can't, I'm paralyzed. My vision blurs in and out, the throbbing in my head returning.

"Lex?" His mouth moves, a deep, husky voice drifting towards me, cutting through all the other noise in the room. His tone is sharp, tugging at memories just out of reach. I know that voice, I know those eyes, but I don't know him. "Is that you?"

He moves towards me, and everything suddenly goes so quiet. My pulse speeds up. A deep-rooted fear settles in my toes and climbs slowly, inch by inch. Limbs grow heavy, body motionless, eyes bonded to his. My mind is reeling. The fear is visceral, but I have no idea what triggered it. Surely not some strange boy at a party. A boy who I've never seen before but who seems to think he knows me.

The longer he stares, the tighter my chest gets. My body stiffens, readying itself for battle. An insistent force drives me to flee, but there's a spark of something else, too. Familiarity. It has been haunting me, trailing after me these past few weeks. A glimpse of knowing, but also not knowing. The desire to run from him, but also run to him. The battle of wills renders me motionless.

His arm reaches out and I already know the warmth I will feel when his skin touches mine. When his hand cradles my chin. When his fingers brush my cheek. The flashes in my head merge with this boy in front of me. I'm not ready to make that real. I don't think I can handle what that could mean. I don't even know what that could mean.

I pulse and itch to run away, blindly stumbling to the door leaving a chemtrail of anxiety behind me. I've stepped out into the sun for the first time. Eyes unfocused, steps uncertain.

But he is following me. The pattern of his feet falls against the hardwood floor after me, inching closer. I wind my way back through the party and towards the front door.

The crowd caves in on me and heat rises through my limbs. Breath short, palms sweaty. The anticipation of finding him at this party replaced with a guttural fear. *Run. Get away. Danger.* He hasn't done anything to provoke this, and yet, it's there, ingrained in me. I have no control over myself; I just know I need to run.

I frantically elbow between the dancing bodies. The music is so loud it seizes my thoughts. My anxiety races ahead of me. I can only focus enough on the surrounding crowd to see the dark hair of the stranger still following.

Hunting.

His eyes plead from across the room, almost desperate. I linger one second too long before pushing through the front door.

"Lex, wait!"

The cool air hits me, immediately sobering, and I stumble a little off the stoop and into the driveway. I turn the corner past a hedge of greenery when a hand grabs my forearm and pulls me around. His touch is a spark, his woodsy scent an invasion; his full moon eyes eclipse me entirely.

"Lex, please..." is all he has time to say before I knee him between the legs and take off running down the open road.

I make it home quickly, albeit sweaty and out of breath. My

heart has slowed, but I'm a tornado of words and feelings and questions.

He's real. The boy from my visions is real. I'm not crazy. But I couldn't even talk to him. The need to run from him was overwhelming. Something triggering inside of me make me desperate to get away from him as quickly as possible.

But he recognized me. That look… he longed for me. That wasn't a look to run from. He was hurt, surprised, and relieved. Relieved to see me, as if I were the missing piece that would put him back together.

Something deep inside stretches, waking up. Something I can't quite make sense of. Something I know is going to turn my world upside down. But my world has already been turned upside down, and I don't know if I can handle anything else—anyone else—doing it again.

My house is dark when I creep through the back door. I find my way to the staircase and up to my bedroom, only turning on the lamp when the door is secured tightly. My bed is made, not how I left it. There on my pillow, neatly folded, is the perfect black shift dress from my mother's closet floor.

# FOURTEEN

**I BARELY SLEPT ALL** night. When it did come for me, faces of people I don't know haunted my dreams, staring at me and studying me. I kept waking in a fit of sweat, needing to steady my breath.

That's why I'm up so damn early. On a Saturday morning.

Who am I?

That is the question, isn't it. It's getting harder to deny that something's wrong with me. Or my head. Or my life. Something doesn't fit. These memories, that boy. Someone who clearly knows me, remembers me, even though I have no idea who he is.

Though that doesn't quite fit either.

I didn't recognize him, but I know him. My body knows him. I can't ignore how he makes me feel. The butterflies that swarmed the moment I saw him. The electricity that bolted through my limbs, tingling down my arms.

Feelings that made me run.

I give my head a shake, trying to knock those feelings loose. Let them bury themselves back from wherever they came from.

I roll over, grab my phone from the nightstand. It's dead. Of course, it's dead. With a groan, I stumble out of bed and fumble for the charger.

The sun is just coming up; I have so much of the day ahead of me. I could crawl back into bed, pray for sleep. I should be a good student and finish my homework. Make Mom proud. But I can't shake last night.

I had all the answers, right there in front of me, and what did I do? I panicked and ran.

Idiot.

Now that I've calmed down and regrouped, I wish I had talked to him. Wish I had done what I went there for. I need to talk to him. See how he knows me. Find some answers.

I stare longingly at my bed, but instead tiptoe across the room and to my closet, yanking open the door. My clothes hang at attention as always; well-pressed school uniforms, shoes all aligned in order on the floor, dresses in soft blues and pinks and yellows.

I groan again. It suddenly feels so difficult to get dressed. To find something to wear. All I want is a worked-in pair of jeans and a comfortable t-shirt. I have to crawl back behind a rainbow of frills until I find something that is even remotely comfortable. I quickly slip into a pair of distressed black jeans and a blank black t-shirt. I grab my purse from the floor and pause at my bedroom door, listening for movement across the hall in my mom's room, but there's nothing.

I take a deep breath before easing it open and then quietly pad down the hall, down the stairs, and into a pair of Chelsea boots. I make sure the front door doesn't slam after me, and only then do I let out the breath I was holding.

The air is crisp and cool, coating my throat as I breathe in. But it's comforting, encouraging. It pushes me into a brisk walk as I head back to Brian's house. I can apologize for how I acted, ask if he wants to go for a walk, finally get the answers I want. The answers I need. Get his name, at the very least.

It's just before 8 am when I get to Brian's and for a minute, I wonder if it's too early to ring. But I don't care. There are more important things than Saturday sleep-ins. I ring the doorbell and wait. The house is quiet, the neighborhood much the same. The sun is peeking over the trees on the heavily lined street. I'm standing on a precipice, and my stomach dips at the thought of what comes next.

The door finally opens to a mess of bedhead and bloodshot eyes.

"Dude, why?" Brian mumbles, rubbing his fist against his eye socket. He's wearing a pair of sweatpants, bare feet, and a ratty old t-shirt that has seen better days. He looks as if he's seen better days.

"Hey Bri, uh, sorry to wake you? But I need to talk to Andy, is he still here?" I try to look past Brian into the house, it's dark and empty, everyone still sleeping it seems.

"Sorry brah, he split early. Had to work." Brian leans against the door, which falls back and clunks into the wall with the weight of holding him.

"Well can you call him or something? It's important," I try again, but Brian's eyes have shut, and he seems to have fallen asleep standing up. "Brian! Your phone?"

He absent-mindedly pats his sweats, eyes still shut, and comes up empty. He gives me a little shrug. "I dunno what happened…" he whispers, the words dragging across his lips. "I gotta go man…" He starts to close the door.

"Wait—his friend, I need to know about his friend."

"He has too many friends." The door keeps closing.

"Well at least tell me where he works. Give me something!" I shove my foot in between the door and the frame, the sudden stop making Brian snap awake, finally.

"Spin Records on Queen West. Later dude." The door shuts, leaving me standing alone on the front porch, about to head off on a wild goose chase.

I reach for my phone to google the store; find the number to call, but my pocket is empty. As is my purse. My phone is sitting back on my nightstand, charging. A lot of good that will do me. I could go back for it, but the city isn't that far, and I'd rather talk to him in person, anyway.

I hoof it to the bus stop at the end of Brian's street. I don't wait long before the proper bus pulls in and I'm settled into a seat at the back.

I'm not one for spontaneous trips to the city, especially

without telling anyone where I'm going. Especially without my phone for reassuring company. I've lost control. A desperate need driving me to find answers, no matter the consequences.

I wring my hands together in my lap, chew my lip, and bounce my leg. Anxiety is coming off me in every direction as I patiently wait for the bus to pull into the city core and let me out. After a kind station employee points me in the right direction, I head toward Queen St. West. Towards the record shop. Towards my future… and my past.

It's a trendy part of the city, so I shouldn't be surprised that there is more than one record shop along that stretch. Eventually I find Spin, the sign hanging over the door stopping me still.

I take a minute to collect myself. Calm my nerves, smooth out my shirt, and then press into the store.

I'm greeted with loud music as soon as I enter. But instead of wincing, I immediately feel at home. Somehow, this has been missing from my life and I didn't even realize it. The store is mostly empty, lined with inviting rows upon rows of vinyl.

I wander aimlessly up and down the aisles, running my fingertips over the different album covers waiting to see what jumps out. The Strokes, Radiohead, The White Stripes—bands that I vaguely recognize, that I must have heard of somewhere along the line. I would bet money that these aren't bands Kayla would ever be listening to though, so I'm not sure where I would have heard them.

"What are you doing here?" A deep voice startles me, and I brace myself for those intense green-gray eyes as I turn around.

My heart drops.

"Andy," I say, trying to hide the disappointment in my tone. I look quickly around the rest of the store, but there's no sign of his friend. "I'm looking for… for your friend, is he here?"

"*He's* back in Clifton Hills looking for *you*. Which is why I'm stuck here covering his shift." His annoyance is palpable.

I roll my eyes, running my hands through my hair. It's knotted and wild; I guess I forgot to comb it. I hate that I'm relieved Logan isn't here to witness this version of me.

"How do you know Logan anyway?" Andy asks, bluntly breaking into my thoughts.

*Logan*. It sends a shudder through me, fits right in with my cracks and seams, filling up the empty space.

"That's what I'm trying to find out," I mumble.

"Well, he seemed pretty shook when he saw you at the party. You break his heart or something? I knew there as a girl from back home who did a number on him, I just didn't realize it was *you*." There's unwarranted hostility in his words that I don't think I deserve. But, really, what do I know.

"Logan's from Clifton Hills?" I ask, unconsciously taking a step closer. Andy leans back against a row of records, putting space between us again.

"What? No, dummy. Colbourne. Isn't that where you lived before? Kayla told me, but I never put it together." Andy's lost in thought, drawing lines between dots that I'm only just realizing exist.

"Logan is from the town I grew up in?" I repeat, like an idiot.

Which is exactly how Any makes me feel with the look he gives me.

"I figured that's why you bolted from the party. Couldn't face the ex whose heart you stomped all over. I tried to drag him back here with me, but he wouldn't leave, not without talking to you. And now, you're here. Leaving him chasing ghosts." He purses his lips, a quirked smile that annoys me to no end. How does Kayla stand this guy?

"Yeah, well, I guess I ought to get back then." I say, backing away from him and heading toward the door. If I can get back to Clifton Hills, I might be able to find Logan before he leaves. "Thanks Andy, you're a real pal." My sarcasm seems lost on him, yet he glares at me as I head back out into the street.

My face is warm; the kind of warmth that accompanies embarrassment, desperation, ridiculousness. I impulsively jumped a bus to the city to track down some boy. That's more a Kayla move, but at least she'd be proud of me.

I start back towards the bus stop, taking in the buildings lining the strip. It's a cool neighborhood and I picture myself coming here once I've graduated. Meeting friends at these trendy bars, seeing shows each night of the week, eating out instead of having to stomach that swill from the cafeteria.

I never thought myself a city girl, but being here in this moment, seeing the potential for a young woman, suddenly my future clicks into place. This is where I want to be. Not stuck back in that town, not working for the Academy, not within the same vicinity as my mother.

The thought stops me mid-stride. I've never thought that before. The need to break free of her and build my own life in my own city. It's thrilling.

I feel lighter. Determined. I have a goal. A future. I know where I'm going.

So, when I reach the bus stop, the café it's in front of throws me for a loop. There's a large sign, a stark white logo with circles and lines. I've never been here before, but I know it. It only takes three beats before I realize from where.

I rifle through my purse, pushing aside all the crap in the bottom until I feel the sharp plastic edge of the guitar pick. Satisfaction settles me as I pull it out. The silver sharpie heart is still there, but on the other side is the same logo as the café.

My body vibrates, tugging me to the café. The bus isn't due for another fifteen minutes, enough time to check it out and still make it back before Logan leaves, hopefully.

It's a bit of a dive, but with a little bit of charm. Wooden booths covered in hand drawn graffiti. A bar and kitchen area to the right. In the back, an open area with a stage. It's too early for anyone to be there other than the brunch crowd. I expect to feel as though I've stepped into a strange land, but instead I feel like I've come home.

I take a few more steps into the café. I look at the abstract art on the walls. Run my hands over the wooden tabletops with names carved into them, and I realize I'm smiling.

"Lex!" A shout from the back of the café.

I look over my shoulder for anyone else, until I realize they're talking to me. Remember that they aren't the first person who has called me Lex, either.

The girl rushes towards me, arms outstretched. Before I can step away, she's pulled me into a warm hug.

"Oh my god, I can't believe you're here. It's been so long!" She pulls back and looks at me expectantly. I don't know what to say. Or do. I don't know who this is.

"Um, hi?" I say weakly. She eyes me suspiciously, hurt masked with annoyance, and then wipes her face clean.

"Where's Logan? I don't think I've ever seen you here without him." She laughs, her comfortable charm returning.

"Oh, I, well I thought he might be here. But I guess not… I'll let you get back to what you were doing." I start to back away, but she grabs my hand, tugging me back towards the stage.

"You can't leave, not until you see the new system we got," she jumps up on stage, taking a natural stance behind the mic. "Helloooooooo," she speaks into it, her voice distorted and ringing aloud into the restaurant.

Customers enjoying their brunch drop cutlery in shock, turning to look back at us.

"Too early, Jess!" One of the servers calls from the front. Jess. That's who this is. Doesn't ring a bell.

"Hey Jess," I say, her name feeling odd in my mouth. "This may sound weird, but when was the last time we were here?" I ask, trying not to sound like an airhead.

Jess laughs heartily. "Don't tell me you were too drunk to remember. It had to be… I don't know, like almost a year? It was just starting to get cold because you were wearing that killer leather jacket I love. Oh wait, I know…" she grabs my arm again, dragging me over to the wall.

It's a gallery wall, different photos of different people scattered in various patterns. The only word that comes to mind is rock 'n' roll. Everyone in the photos is either performing on the stage to my left or standing in a crowd cheering. There are even more group shots of pierced and tatted and leather-clad people.

At the end of one row, where Jess is pointing, I see a flash of red hair. My hair. Only in this photo, it's pulled back slick at the sides into a faux hawk that cascades over my right shoulder. My eyes are lined heavily with a black cat's eye. And attached to my face, lips pursed against my cheek, is a boy. A familiar boy.

"There we go, you and Logan, the last night you were here. We put it up because you hadn't come back in a while, and we weren't sure when you would. We tried to get in touch with him to book another show, but he never returned our calls."

I have no words.

At this point, I'm not surprised to see me in the same frame as him. All clues point to knowing him. But I have no memory of this night. I bring my fingers to my cheek, gently running the tips over the surface his lips graced in the photo. Such intimacy.

"You'll tell him he's missed, yeah? Tell him to come back and see us!" Jess says eagerly.

I nod, dumbfounded. "Yeah, of course. Sure. Sorry, I have to run. But it was good to see you… again." I turn and hurry past the tables and back out into the street just as the bus is pulling up.

# FIFTEEN

**THE BUS RIDE HOME** was long but quiet. I made it home just as dusk started to settle and managed to sneak back upstairs without detection. I briefly wonder whether my mom even noticed I was gone. And then I wonder whether she would have cared. Again, thoughts sprouting from a deep, dark place I haven't visited before, but they don't shock me. They seem accurate.

I waited for him to come to our house. He didn't.

I waited for him to call. He couldn't, without my number.

I waited for a sign or a clue or something that would bring us together. Something that would tell me where he was, how we were connected, why he suddenly showed up in my life again, but nothing presented itself.

I scrolled through my phone, all my missed messages from Kayla and Hannah after the party. Lurked through Instagram to see if anyone needed damage control after that party. Anyone other than me, I guess.

And I fantasized. A lot. About who this boy was to me. Who he could be. If I'd run into him again. Where he could have gone. Would he come back? It was enough to drive a girl crazy. Eventually I shut off my phone and buried myself under my duvet.

That's what they call self-care.

When Monday morning rolls around, I pull my head out of my fantasy bubble and prepare to set foot back in the real world again. Prepare to face-off with my mom again.

After the way we left things Friday night, I ready myself for a field of landmines as I inch my way down the stairs. But it's just her in the kitchen. Standing there as she always does, cooking breakfast, and humming quietly to herself.

"There you are. I thought you were going to oversleep. You look wiped." So, we're back to playing house. She tosses a tea towel onto the counter and moves closer to inspect me. "Are you feeling okay?"

Where do I start? I take a seat and pour some orange juice into a glass, putting all my energy into not spilling it all over the table. I want to tell her everything. To confide in her as I used to when I was a little girl frightened awake from a nightmare. Because this has to be a nightmare. Not real. A strange boy showing up, haunting me. As if he knows me.

But he does know me. And I know him. I took pictures with him at a café we visited often. I let him press his lips against me. And I enjoyed it. I know I enjoyed it.

"Kayla called for you, a few times. She said she couldn't get through on your phone. Don't tell me you've lost it again, Alexandra."

"It died," I mumble, patting my pocket to make sure it's there. It's warm to the touch, even through the fabric of my slacks. Freshly charged.

"Well, she sounded worried. Is everything alright?" Her eyes squint, studying me. She's speaking light but careful. Trying to tease something out of me. I'm thrown. I was expecting a lecture, scolding, disappointment. But she's playing nice. Too nice. I wonder if Kayla told her anything about the party, about me running off. But if she knows anything more, she doesn't ask.

"I'm fine," I manage, spooning some eggs onto my plate so I have something to shove in my mouth to end this conversation.

"Nothing happened?" she asks, clearly not believing me. I shake my head, pointing to my mouth and then to my watch. I shove my plate away and grab my bag from the front stoop where I last left it. "As long as you're sure everything is okay. You know you can talk to me about anything." And I wish that were true.

She trails me to the door, hovering. It must take all she has not to grab me and stop me from leaving her with nothing. I wish her a good day over my shoulder and quickly close the door.

⁜⁜⁜⁜

"But you, like, disappeared," Kayla says, her arms waving wildly. They're waiting for me at the school gates, as usual, only with more ammo. Berating me with questions the minute I approach.

"You were standing there one second, and then poof! Gone. I texted you. I called you. A few times." She folds her arms together across her chest, hitching out her hip. If her foot starts tapping, then I'll really feel like a scolded child.

We make our way through the crowded hallway and settle into our seats for first period. The bell hasn't rung yet, and students linger around, dissecting their weekends. Some of them were at the party Friday night, though no one seems to have noticed me bolting out the front door. Or at least if they did, they don't seem to care. Not as much as Kayla.

"We didn't know if you were okay," Hannah adds, her quiet input always a little heartbreaking. The guilt is immediate. I want to explain, I want to tell them what came over me, but I don't even know how to explain it to myself.

"Look, I'm sorry. I didn't feel good. I didn't have much for dinner and the beer was warm, it turned my stomach. I had to get some fresh air." Now I'm waving my arms wildly, trying to make the whole thing lighter and more believable, but they both stare at me.

"Logan was right miffed when he got back." Kayla treads cautiously, but she's deliberately pushing me for information. My heart skips at his name and I'm sure my face immediately flushes.

"Who is Logan?" I play dumb, batting my eyes innocently.

"Andy's mate? The bloke we saw you leaving with. You know, the one who was calling you by a nickname like he's known you for years?" Kayla's raised eyebrows get more pointed, her lips thinning out. "Which, by the way, is bullshit. You get pissed when

I call you Lexi or even Alex, and yet this guy, who you have never once mentioned, can call you Lex? What's the deal, *Alexandra*?" Her sass makes my full name splatter like roadkill.

"I don't know who he is." I start, but thankfully the bell rings and our teacher trudges into the room, sucking all the noise and idle movements out of it.

Kayla lets out a frustrated sigh as she settles into her chair, slowly drawing her suspicious eyes away from me and towards the front of the room. Mine, however, stay gazing out the window into the yard to the West of the school. The edge of the front gate is visible. Follow the stone wall that lines the property until it crawls up close to the cliff's edge.

The lake is narrow here. It's not far to the other side. The water could easily carry me there, away from here. Body sprawled out, floating on the waves. A sea of small hands, gently cradling me as I ebb and flow with the current.

Kids jump off the cliff all the time. It's become a dare for the upperclassmen. Especially since apparently the woman who lives directly across the lake sits on her porch every night with the cops on speed dial. Highlight of her night is when one of us hooligans pop up on her property.

I'm planning my watery escape when a loud squeak radiates through the open classroom door as sneakers come to a hurried stop outside. Everyone looks, but only I seem to recognize him. Logan. Here, at my school. Staring at me again with those imploring eyes.

Messy dark hair keeps falling across his face, that tattooed arm brushing it aside. Instead of our school uniform, he's in a pair of ripped jeans and a plaid shirt over a tee with *The Strokes* etched on the front. A much better uniform, I'd say.

"Can I help you?" Mr. Robinson has seen him now, too. He clears his throat, straightening his tie in an act to be professional and authoritative, but he's noticed the tension.

"I need to talk to Lex." Logan's voice tries to be smooth and confident, but he's clearly out of breath. Mr. Robinson's glare pins him to the doorframe, but he keeps glancing over his shoulder, waiting for someone.

"Lex? You mean Alexandra? Miss Shaw is in the middle of class; you are going to have to leave before I call security." It's a threat, but by the sounds echoing in the hallway, security is already on the way. Logan keeps wiping at his forehead, brushing the hair away but also sweat that's building there. I can taste his anxiety as he wavers in the doorway. He's running out of time.

"No, not Shaw, Lex Holland," he says an unfamiliar name, but he keeps staring at me. "Lex, please, I need to talk to you. Please!"

My chest aches. I want to run to him instead of from him. Desperation makes his voice crack, and an invisible tether pulls at me, begging me to go to him. But I don't, I can't. Despite my betraying body, the screaming in my gut, I don't know who this boy is. So, I just sit there, staring blankly. Dumbly.

Eyes bounce back and forth between us until Security barges into the standoff, grabbing him across his chest from behind. He digs his fingers into the doorframe, nails bending from the force as if they'll give him more strength to hang on.

"They told me you were dead!" He yells, moving his shoulders back and forth to knock the guards off him. Their arms pull harder, his eyes bulging wider. "Lex, you are supposed to be dead!" Words loud as day, but there's a buzzing in my ears and my vision flutters in and out. In and out.

One guard reaches for the baton at his hip. It all happens in slow motion. In and out of focus. The baton rises above the guard's head and then smashes across Logan's fingers as they cling to the doorframe. The knuckles split open, blood bursts from the wound and splatters against the white wall.

His face cringes in pain, a pain I can almost feel myself as my stomach drops out and my breath catches. The baton goes up again and down again on the other hand. The other guard yanks him from the doorway and into the hall with a sickening rip.

There's an insufferable sticky sound against the floor, boots shuffling and grown men huffing out energy they were not expecting to expel on a Monday morning. There's a low moan that must be him, the sound thinning as they drag him down the hallway.

Mr. Robinson slowly walks to the door and closes it, returning to put marker to the whiteboard and start today's lesson as if nothing happened.

# SIXTEEN

**"I HEARD HE ESCAPED** from a mental institute and hitchhiked his way here."

"I heard his brother Lex was killed in a hunting accident and he went mad with grief."

"I heard *he* killed his brother before he tried to kill himself and then came into the school to kill us."

"That doesn't even make sense!" I slam my locker shut, and it echoes through the hallway. "He ran into the school to kill us, with no weapons, after he tried to kill himself. What is wrong with you?"

The three freshmen freeze in front of me, their books held up like a shield. It doesn't stop me from glaring at them in disgust.

"You baby twats should probably get before he comes back to find you," Kayla mocks from behind them, and they scurry off. I am grateful for her presence, but I can't meet her eyes; I don't know what they're going to hold. Instead, I stare at her lips, pursed as she studies me. Like she has no idea who I am. She and me both.

"What's going on with you?" Her question is kind and light, her protective hostility chasing after the freshmen and leaving me with the softness she reserves for her best friend. For me.

"I don't know." It's a whisper, and mostly the truth.

"Look, I know I haven't been the best friend in the last little bit. I've been so preoccupied with my own shit. But you can talk to me, you know. You don't have to keep everything to yourself…" She trails off, and that's when I hear it. The hurt in her voice. She always has such a strong, confident front, but the foundation is cracking.

"I know, Kay. It's not like that. I don't even, I can't..." I don't have the words. I'm already struggling to put them together for myself. Where do I even start? "I don't know him," I whisper.

"Well, he bloody well seems to know you."

"I don't think I know him. I didn't know his name, I didn't know his face, but he felt familiar, somehow. When I saw him across the room at the party, I couldn't breathe. I had to get out of there. I haven't been able to stop thinking of him. I haven't slept. I don't know what is happening to me."

I huff out a breath, kicking at the floor with my shoe, trying to distract from the anxiety I felt that night. But Kayla doesn't laugh, doesn't tell me I'm overreacting. Her face is pensive, as if she's trying to solve a math problem.

"He said you died. I mean, that's bollocks, right?" I think I nod, but it is such a subtle movement that she asks me again. "Right?"

"I don't know! I mean, of course, I didn't die. I'm standing right in front of you. I bleed, I cry, I'm not a robot. Feel, I'm not a ghost." I throw out my arms as proof but retract them before she can even pretend to touch. "I'm not the undead. I don't want to eat your brains."

The humor is lost on us because with every joke I make, the answers seem to slip further away. "You don't think he..." *Went wild*, is what I want to say, but I hold the thought still on my tongue because I'm afraid to suggest it.

I think back to Friday morning. Kyle Larson running wild outside the cafeteria. The stories that haunt our hallways. About Emily Tran and other students having an episode and then disappearing.

But it can't be that. Logan doesn't even go here. What he's saying can't be true, either, because I didn't die. I'm right here, very much alive. And I have never seen him before in my life.

The door across the hall from us opens. Headmaster Johnson's office. I expect his large frame to step through the opening, but it's my mother who steps out instead. Her eyes widen at the sight of me, but she quickly pulls her features back to her usual stoic expression.

"Alexandra." She nods at me, then Kayla.

"Mother." I return her nod and say nothing more, making the moment incredibly awkward. I don't have to guess what she was doing in Headmaster Johnson's office after what just happened. I stand tall, challenging her to reprimand me, to do *something*. It's so bizarre when your two worlds collide—my home life, standing within my school life. The universe as torn, and I exist but don't exist at the same time.

"You ruined my life, you know," she finally says. She may as well be talking through a glass window; I can barely make out the words.

"What?" I ask, the same sense of dread building in my stomach as the other day.

"I said you're going to be late, you know. For class? The bell is about to ring." She squints at me, eyebrows furrowed. She doesn't trust me, and for a minute, I don't trust myself. I'm standing in this hallway but have one foot somewhere else entirely.

She doesn't say a proper goodbye, just turns on her heel, and walks towards the exit at the other end of the hall. My eyes follow her. My head dwells on the conversation. I couldn't have misheard her, could I? I'm losing my mind.

I don't even hear Hannah approach she's so quiet. "Well?" Kayla nods at her in greeting, but Hannah's concentrating on a set of tarnished industrial keys. She peels one off before tucking them back into her backpack alongside her schoolbooks and a bunch of loose colored papers.

"They're holding him in the basement. I have never been down there before today, have you? Long, dusty hallways and lots of closed doors. But he's there, the last door on the right. You'll need this to get down there." She hands me the key.

"Where did you... how do you know?" I stare at her in disbelief and she just shrugs. "I can't barge in there. Those mall cops will stop me before I even get close. Wait, why would I even go near him? You saw him, he's deranged, he's gone wild. This isn't right."

I started pacing without realizing it, my thoughts a mind-numbing game of ping pong in my head. Kayla and Hannah watch me, leaning against the lockers, looking as helpless as I feel.

"When he chased you from that party and came back alone, I could have ripped his throat out," Kayla starts, Hannah nodding emphatically in agreement. "But he *knows* you, Alexandra. He was inconsolable, absolutely shattered. Muttering about an accident, about a girl who died. Maybe you look like her, or remind him of her, but I don't think he's mad. Don't you want to know why he thought you were dead?"

"That's all I want! I want to know where this guy came from, why he says he knows me. I want to know why my mother has been acting so weird lately. I want to know what is happening to me. Why I keep having flashes of things I can't make sense of. Why I'm sleepwalking through my life like it's not my own," I exclaim, frustration taking hold.

What I don't admit is that I need to put words to the magnetic pull towards this stranger. Discover why I feel I've known him my entire life. Truth is, the minute he showed up at my classroom door, I realized I was waiting for him ever since that party.

My instinct to run from him was a knee-jerk reaction based on the flood of overwhelming emotions. But underneath that was something more grounding, more familiar. Something I trust. And that is telling me I know him. I don't recognize him. I don't remember him. But I know him, and I need to know how.

"We think you should hear him out," Hannah adds, shrugging.

I sigh at the key in my hand. There's no way I can go back to class now.

# SEVENTEEN

**HANNA ISN'T WRONG; THE** basement is creepy. Chipping cement stairs descend into a mass of darkness. A dank, moldy smell climbs into each pore. I feel grimy the minute I step through the door.

Hannah wanted to come with me but sneaking into a locked basement is going to be hard enough without another body to account for. Though when I slipped the key into the lock and turned, I couldn't help but think that I was wildly unprepared for...for what? I'm not sure what my plan is. Sneak in and talk to him? That is, if I can even make it there without being caught.

I pull out my phone and turn on the flashlight, which gives a hyper focused spotlight on the scene in front of me. My shoes pad quietly along the cement floor. A dim light at the end of the hallway guides me, but the rest of it melts into the shadows. The light on my phone brushes over large and ominous doors; solid slabs of concrete, no windows, no markings. There's no sound behind them, nothing but my own breathing.

As I get closer to the end of the hall, I realize the dim light is a lamp sitting on a desk in a small glassed-in office. There's no movement in the office, but I approach cautiously.

To my right is a door. I can't tell it apart from all the others, Hannah said it's the one I am looking for. To my left is a smaller door with a fading zigzag symbol on it.

I try the handle of the door to my right, but it's locked. I try the key Hannah gave me, but it doesn't even go into the lock. I'm trying to be quiet, but the key makes a scraping noise as I try to force it in. There's movement behind the door in response.

*Think... think...* I try the office door and it's also locked, but now that I'm closer, I can see what I need hanging inside on the wall. Keys. They are assigned numbers, like in a motel, but it's hard to know what door they belong to. I must have passed six or seven on each side of the hallway leading down here. All of them unmarked.

I take off my blazer and wrap it around my elbow before slamming it into the glass of the door. It gives surprisingly easily, making a louder shatter than I would have liked, and my adrenaline kicks in. I wait for an alarm, but security seems to put all their faith in the locked basement door and no one comes running.

I drop the blazer and quickly slip my arm past the broken glass to unlock it. The eerie glow from the lamp is enough to paw through the personal effects strewn across the desk: a calendar dated three years ago, a pencil with defined teeth marks etched in, a chipped white mug stained a putrid brown. I open and close a few drawers until I come to one full of loose files. Shuffling through them quickly, they are clearly student files. Most have names I don't recognize, but then there is one that I do.

### Tran, Emily

When I open it, I'm met with the vacant eyes of a young girl with a long dark braid slung over one shoulder. She's smiling, but it's crooked. One corner tugged up unnaturally, unbalanced. She's leering past the camera, which makes her almost ethereal, but there's something familiar about her. I recognize her, though I haven't met her before. I can't stomach the idea of another forgotten memory, so I tear my eyes away to the other pages. Medical documents and a couple of newspaper clippings. I keep flipping until bright red ink smeared across the page stops me.

### Deceased

I tear into the other files, the same bright red stamp on the last page confirming their tragic fates. These must be the files of the students who have gone wild. There's at least five in the drawer, I don't even want to think about how many may be in those filing cabinets.

These rooms must be where they hold students after removing them from the school. Whisked away and remembered only as ghost stories around the fire.

One file has handwritten ink on the tab instead of a computer-printed label. It stands out against the rest as the most recently added. I don't need to pull it out to know what it will say.

Larson, Kyle – TBD

A shiver runs through me. They work quickly. Whisking students away, their fate undetermined. I don't have time to consider whether Kyle might be behind one of these cement doors. The horrible click of a door being unlocked echoes against the cement walls. Adrenaline slams back into me as bright streams of light shine into the dark hallway at the other end. Someone is coming.

I grab a handful of motel keys and duck out of the office before I cast a shadow through the desk lamp. The slow and careless footsteps are moving slowly, they have a lot of ground to cover, but I still have to work fast.

As quietly as I can, I slip one key after another into the lock of the door to the right, willing it to turn. When one does, I push it open quickly and gaze into a completely dark cell.

"Logan—" I whisper-yell, laying the keys down at my feet softly. There is a rustling in the far corner, and I freeze. What if Hannah's wrong? "I swear, if I just locked myself in a cell with… who knows what…" I mutter to myself. But then I catch a whiff of that woodsy smell and relief floods through me.

His hands find me in the dark, landing on my shoulders. They slide down until they are engulfing my small hands, leaving a tingling trail down my arms. Each one of his fingertips press into mine—strange but also welcome. Grounding.

I'm surprisingly calm, alone in a cell with an unknown boy. My gut screams at me again, a metal detector, shrill and magnetized. We say nothing, but my racing heart says everything.

There's a soft whistle coming down the hall, but it is moving haltingly, pausing outside each of the doors as it grows closer. Gripping his hand tighter, I lead us both back towards the door, easing it back open.

The desk lamp is flickering, providing enough light for me to see across from us, but not much further. Now that I'm staring at it, I realize the image on the front of that door isn't a zigzag; it's a symbol for stairs.

I have no way of knowing whether it's locked, but it's our only way out—there's no getting passed whoever is coming down the hallway. Our only hope is that we'll have a big enough head start to make it wherever those stairs lead before someone catches us or calls for backup.

I inhale deeply. His voice is in my ear, soft and reassuring, "I'm right behind you." That is all I need to push me forward. We dart across the hall and through the yellowing light towards the door. Within the flurry of our movement, the person down the hall perks up and runs.

There's yelling and the hiss of a radio, but we're already pushing through the other door. We run up a set of cement stairs, taking them two at a time. It's a stretch for my small legs, and my thighs ache, but I keep climbing, Logan right on my heels.

The stairs spiral up and up more flights than I took down, but we finally reach a big red emergency door with a push bar. I slam into it, begging it to be open, as Logan pushes up behind me.

It gives away, a siren screaming in alarm as we fall out into the bright, sunlit afternoon. I try to catch my breath and place my surroundings, but Logan finds my hand again and we keep running.

There's a wet spray on the wind, and I realize we're behind the school and heading towards the forest. We reach the tree line and duck in among the greenery.

The door at the back of the school bursts open again, and the security guard tumbles out. He has one hand on his baton and the other on his radio, panicked words floating through the air but getting lost before they reach us.

The forest pulls us in tighter as we turn our backs and hurry further into its arms.

# EIGHTEEN

**WE RUN UNTIL I'M** winded and need to stop and catch my breath. I lean up against a tree, doubling over as I take in big, deep gasps.

"Lex. You're not dead." His words take effort, pushed out through jagged breaths, but I know it's not just because of our sprint through the forest. There's a different pain gripping them tightly, making sharp cuts as he forces them out.

"I'm not dead," I answer simply. I have outrun everything I thought I knew and am an empty shell, hovering at the creek's edge. I have no grasp of what is going on, who I am, why there are students kept in cells in the basement of my school.

"When I saw you at that party, I thought, I didn't know what to think. I couldn't go back to uni without knowing for sure. But how? I mean, what happened? I waited for you, and you never showed. Then the news, and the accident. I was at your funeral,

Lex."

"My name isn't Lex, why are you calling me Lex?" That's what I ask, but what I want to know is what he's talking about. Waited for me where? What funeral?

"I've always called you Lex," he says, as if I'm the one talking nonsense.

As it goes quiet, I have the chance to study him. His eyes I'm already familiar with, but the rest of his features also seem familiar. The hint of facial hair lining a sharp jaw. Not overly muscular, but solid. Larger than me, but he seems to follow similar curves. If I were to press up against him, I'd fit right into him perfectly.

His hands, nestled under the coal-like tattoo of a forest, are worn in and calloused. But I can't forget how soft they felt as they held mine. He towers over me, but it's his natural stance includes a slight bend, so he's gazing right into my eyes.

"You don't know who I am." His words shatter me a bit. They are so heavy with hurt, loss, and grief. His face is noticeably vacant, eyes rimmed red. It makes my breath stop. I want to wrap him in my arms and reassure him that of course I know him—how could I not—but that isn't true. I have no idea who he is.

I pace back and forth between the trees, running my hands through my hair, taking in the gravity of what just happened. This strange boy. Cells in our basement. Chased by security. No, I don't know who he is, but I need to know.

"We need to keep moving." He urges, motioning with his head for me to lead the way. But I'm rooted in place.

"I'm not going anywhere with you until you tell me who you are." I say firmly, though I don't feel as calm or demanding as I sound.

"I think, instead, I should tell you who *you* are." He offers me a sad smile and I get the feeling he knows something I don't.

"I know who I am. I'm not the one who showed up out of nowhere claiming I'm dead," I pant. The mixture of running, of this strange boy materializing in my life, of everything pressing down around me is strangling the breath from me.

He moves his arm out, as if for comfort, and then thinks better of it. His black tree-line tattoo is haunting my peripheral, taunting me. Everything feels surreal, this figure from my mind, my visions, my memories, suddenly standing right next to me.

"Who are you?" I huff out between panicked breaths. "Why are you here?"

The sun is shining down through the treetops, the rays a strobe light. Everything around me is moving in slow motion, robotic. My rapid heartbeat takes on a steadier rhythm, accompanying the music playing in the distance.

The pressure builds behind my eyes again, my head throbbing. I squint, pressing my palms into my eye sockets so that when I open them again, there are white spots everywhere and I'm transported again. To that night at the concert. The photo of us kissing. His smell overtaking me.

"I remember you..." I whisper, shutting my eyes. "I remember you, but I don't know you." The woods are quiet around me, as if remembering my forgotten history as intently as I am. I can't figure out what to say. Memories of that night are wildly unraveling inside of me.

I fish through my purse absentmindedly, grabbing for the junk gathering at the bottom. My hands wrap around the small piece of plastic, and I hold it out to him. The guitar pick, with a silver heart drawn on it.

"That's mine," he smiles, the edge of his lips curving up just slightly at the end. His eyes bore into mine and I suddenly I know the feeling of being on stage. Of everyone staring at me. While I'm naked. A brief flicker of hope comes alive in him.

"No, it's mine. You gave it to me…" I say hesitantly, and he nods. He is barely breathing. Not risking that the subtle movement of his chest would send me scurrying away. There's a gentleness in the way he waits for me to rebuild a girl he knows, a girl I have no memory of.

I take this moment, wrap it tightly around me, and let it breathe new life into me.

A branch breaks in the distance, echoing through the woods and it snaps me back to reality. We just ran from security. From a school where clearly there's more going on than I can even imagine. They are not going to just let us leave.

"Come on, we need to keep moving," I say, starting through the forest again. I feel calmer. The panic and emotion that built up has leveled out, but my mind is flipping wildly. Image after image. The Italian restaurant. The rich spaghetti. The concert. Skipping Junior Prom for our own anti-prom. Holding hands. Listening to music. His lips. Against my lips. In many visions, many different places. Many, many snippets, all of him.

This isn't just a boy I met at a concert. An acquaintance I nodded to in passing. There were many nights. Weeks, maybe even months to account for. My body tugs me towards him. My heart aches, being this close to him. Sewing itself back together again.

The more blank pages he fills up, the more my story will come back to me.

"So, we…." I take a breath, my cheeks burning. I'm acting like a child passing a note, asking him to circle yes or no. "Were we…" He notices my cue and saves me.

"We were dating, yeah." His smile is soft, reassuring. There's history in his eyes. A vault of memories all his own, and I want to pry it open and let everything he knows about me come pouring out. Because the comfort he has with me, the affection that is coming off him in waves, I can't match it. I don't feel it. Maybe I did, at some point, but I just met this boy. My vault is empty.

"How long?" I can barely hear my own voice. The idea that I was with someone, it's a simple concept, a natural conclusion, but it's so strange to me. This me, who has never so much as kissed a boy. Who has always kept her distance from any relationship.

"About eight months." His words are quiet, but the broken pieces cut all the same.

I stumble to a stop. I can't process the fact that I spent eight months with this person, and I don't know anything about him. How is that possible? I'm raking through my memories, trying to sew together all these fragments.

He's standing close to me; the space between us has somehow evaporated. My senses scream at me, my body betrays me, wants to reach out and touch him. I take a deep breath to calm myself and inhale that woodsy scent that I've started associating with him.

A wave of familiarity crashes over me and that's when I remember the rest of it. That's when our eight months together comes flooding back, filling me with a happiness I haven't felt in the longest time.

*A perfect summer. High sun, warm, but not too hot. Long days strolling hand in hand through the woods, dipping toes into the river. Long nights laying underneath the stars, sharing stories and hopes and dreams. Ice cream dripping over fingers. Movies in the park. Picnics by the lake. And music. So, so much music.*

Memories of this boy and me. Logan. Who isn't a stranger at all, but someone I shared so much of my life with.

How could I not know him?

The forest is on fire, a heat like no other. But no, it's not the forest, it's me. An unbearable heat flowing through my body. A redness creeps up my neck and over my cheeks. It spreads rapidly through me as the memories of this boy, this relationship, settle back into my mind. I was in love. I was happy. I wasn't alone.

I'm struck with so many emotions. Lightning rendering me motionless. One minute I'm a girl at a new school with the length of a football field between her and everyone else. The next, I'm flooded with feelings for a stranger in front of me who isn't a stranger at all.

"How could I have forgotten all that? How could I have forgotten you?" The words fall from my mouth in bits and pieces, and I don't know what to do with them. I remember it all so clearly now. Memories that are too precious to have lost.

"And here I thought I was unforgettable." Logan tries to lighten the mood, but it falls flat. He reaches out a steady hand to me and my body wants to move towards him, to fall into his arms, but I make myself pull back. A wave of hurt passes over his face, but he's quick to mask it.

"Maybe it's residual memory loss from the accident. I hit my head pretty hard. Maybe it knocked you right out of it. The doctors told me there are cases of amnesia after car accidents..." I trail off because that doesn't seem right. This isn't a lingering side effect from my head trauma. But I have no other answers and the forest falls quiet.

"We should probably keep going," Logan's voice cuts in and I shake myself out of my confusion.

"Where are we supposed to go?" I wonder aloud, but it's clear that the only answer is anywhere but here. We start moving, quickly and quietly, though the sounds of my heart, the swirl of my thoughts, are turned up to eleven.

Muscle memory kicks in and I realize my feet are heading towards home.

# NINETEEN

**IT'S STARTING TO GET** darker, and the forest has taken on a different feel. Or maybe that's me as my old life spills out over my new one, blurring all the lines. We took the long way through the forest, which spit us out at the top of the road by my house. Home, with my mother and her resentment and all of those memories, is the last place I want to be. Who knows what she will do, knowing I've basically broke a boy out of school jail. But I need some supplies and somewhere to think about what to do next.

The driveway is empty; the house looking the same. We go in through the back door to be safe and don't turn on any of the lights.

"With any luck, my mother is caught up in the chaos at the school. We should have some time to grab some stuff and get out of here." I don't know why I'm whispering when no one else is home, but it seems safer.

"You know, this is the second time I've snuck into your house." There's a smile in his voice as he tiptoes behind me, through the kitchen, up the stairs and into my bedroom. His comment confuses me at first, but then I remember the night he's speaking of.

*Logan frozen in the middle of my room, looking like he was caught pocketing a candy bar. I couldn't help but laugh. This ghostly knight, climbing through my window, thinking he could rescue me. I pulled my covers down, invited him closer. And we talked about everything.*

"Sneaking through people's windows. What are you, a kid from a CW show? Seriously, who does that?" I manage, chuckling to cover the real memory of that night. He wasn't just sneaking in through the window to check on me for no reason. Fear swirls in my stomach and I know that it wasn't a good conversation. I'm too scared to ask him. Did he break my heart? Is he the reason we moved here?

Logan doesn't notice my tension. He just laughs, his breath so warm on my neck it makes my body burn.

We push through my bedroom door, and I immediately start rifling through my belongings for a change of clothes and a black canvas crossbody purse. My closet is as it always is, a rainbow of blush colors, but there is nothing here that I want to reach for. Nothing feels right. But I'm not dressing for a date. I'm trying to get out of here fast as I can. I grab a white t-shirt and a pair of jeans and hope I won't feel too much like an impostor.

I unbutton my blouse, completely forgetting that I'm not alone until Logan gently clears his throat and looks away. He takes in the surroundings of my room with more attention than anyone should. I flush, quickly changing out of my uniform.

I grab a few hair elastics, a pen. I have no idea what I'm doing, but I make a point of putting the guitar pick with the sharpie heart into my bag. It's a talisman now, something I can cling to. Something I lost but have found again.

"Where is everything?" Logan asks me, turning around now that the coast is clear.

"What do you mean?"

"Your room, it's so empty. Before, your old room—there were books piled high on every available surface, records spread out across the floor. Your walls were covered in sketches…" He trails off and I see what he sees: stark white walls devoid of any personality. A reflection of me, devoid of any personality.

"I don't draw," I answer, distracted.

"You did. You called yourself an artist. You drew all over everything: walls, shoes, notebooks, benches. My hands were constantly covered in pencil from being close to you."

I'm suddenly as flat as a piece of paper. Not even a piece of notebook paper, which at least has lines on it, some definition. But a plain white piece of paper with no depth or experience. No hobbies, no interests. No memory of ever going to concerts, of drawing, of him.

I say nothing and instead search for my wallet. I abandoned

my messenger bag back at school, but I rarely take the wallet with me. When I find it, I open it up, but there are only a couple of small bills in it. We won't get far on that. I throw my phone into my purse. What else might I need if I'm about to, I don't know, go on the run?

A shiver runs through me, and I rub my hands over my bare arms. I can't tell if the room is cold or if the events of today are catching up to me, but it doesn't matter. Logan notices. Of course, he does. He slips off the long-sleeved plaid shirt he's wearing and holds it out to me. The gesture is enough to warm me, but I reach out my arms and let him pull the shirt up over my shoulders.

"There, now you look like you," his smile sends a jolt of electricity through me. The weight of his shirt presses against my skin like I want him to. I shake the thought away, turning back to my bag, though I'm finding it harder to focus.

I clear my throat, getting back to the task at hand. "Come on, we need to get out of here before my mom gets home. We need a plan."

"I don't have much, I left my stuff with Andy to take back to campus, but this is everything I have." Logan throws some change and a couple of bills on my bed. He has a train ticket back to Toronto, his escape back to normal, away from all this. Because this doesn't affect him. Not if he doesn't want it to. "Maybe you can come with me, back to campus? Away from here?"

I hadn't thought of that. I could leave this behind, leave my mother, leave whatever is happening. We could run away and start a life together. Find jobs. Find a home. Grow up without any of this hanging over our heads.

The offer is tempting. The dream is even more hypnotizing. But there's a twinge in my gut. A need to know what is happening. Why they're keeping students in the basement, why people are disappearing and going wild. Why I have a whole life I can't seem to remember.

"I can't," I whisper. Logan nods. I think he was expecting that answer. An awkward silence falls between us. "I need to know what is happening to me. Why I forgot you. There has to be something else going on." My stomach coils.

"Do you have any idea what hospital you were at?" Logan asks. "Maybe they have a medical file or more details about how bad things were and what went on while you were there?"

"My mother might have something tucked away in her office."

Logan follows me down the hall to the small office. It's been a long time since I've been in here; there's been no reason to. The room is dark, minimal. Just a small desk and bookshelves that are weirdly lacking books.

I head straight for the desk, rifling through the few items that are scattered across the top. There's a computer keyboard, but no laptop. An agenda open to July, but nothing written on any of the dates. A few paperclips sitting in a pile.

"What are we looking for?" Logan asks, skimming across the few books that line the shelves.

"I don't even know. Medical receipts? Do you even get a receipt when you spend time in a hospital?" I have no idea but continue to open drawers. "I don't even think my mother uses this office. There's nothing here but empty post it pads and capped pens." I hold one up as proof.

The desk has multiple drawers, each one as disappointing as the last, except for the last one on the bottom right. When I pull that one, it jams.

"Is it stuck?" Logan asks, rounding the desk to stand beside me.

"Locked, I think." There's a not-so-subtle keyhole at the top of it. Logan lifts up the keyboard searching for a key but comes up empty.

"Here, let me." He pulls a Swiss Army knife from his pocket. I eye him with some amusement, and he shrugs. "What? It has a bottle opener on it. University necessities."

I step aside as he shoves the end of the knife portion into the keyhole and jiggles. It doesn't take long for it to click open.

"Not exactly Fort Knox, huh." He laughs, moving back so that I can look through the contents.

It may not be Fort Knox, but the find is still gold.

Inside is a photograph. My mother, her brown hair cut short, a smile plastered to her lips as she sits in my father's lap. His hair is floppy; a bushy mustache is nestled over a lopsided grin. And then me, I must be four or five, curled up in my mother's lap. A pile-on family photo. This is how I remember them from when I was younger, before I ruined everything.

"After the accident, things never felt right. My relationship with my mother is so strained now. She hates me because of what

I did to my dad, though she always pretends nothing is wrong anytime I try to ask her about it." The emotions are taking over again, tears pressing against the back of my eyes as I think about him. About the life that we could have had if I hadn't got behind the wheel that day. If I paid more attention.

"Wait, what you did to your dad?" Logan's question jars me, heaves all my guilt and pain up to the surface. For a minute, I'm dizzy and I need to lean against the desk for balance.

"I killed my father," I manage. "He was in the car with me, in the accident. We were on the way back home when I hit a deer. He didn't make it."

Horror contorts his face, and my heart shrivels. He must think I'm a monster. Killing my own father. Shame takes hold of my body again, shaking it slightly, constricting my breath. I back away from him slowly, afraid of the vile words that might come out of his mouth next. The same words my mother whispers. The blame, the hate.

"Lex—" his voice isn't coarse; it's soft and soothing, like he's trying to talk me off a ledge. "That isn't what happened. You didn't kill your father."

My entire world stops. His words clang through my mind, a bullet ricocheting off my skull.

"That's… not possible. I see the accident every time I close my eyes. The blame and hatred anytime my mother speaks to me. I remember it so clearly, Logan. My chest ripping open when I saw him in the passenger seat, covered in red, not moving, not breathing."

"No, Lex. None of that is true," He pauses, and everything stops. His face falls as he tries to figure out how to form the next words. "You weren't driving, Lex. Your mother was."

The memory throws me against a wall, and I shatter. My entire existence bursting into pieces.


*We're in the car—the three of us. Rain threatening to fall, the sky a purplish black. I'm supposed to be meeting Logan and am trying to text him to let him know I'm running late, but my phone has no signal.*

*They're arguing. It's all they do lately. About him leaving, again.*

*"Why are you like this?" My voice cracks from the back seat, the words desperate. There are tears bursting over the rims of my eyes, leaving streaks on my cheeks that match the rain on the windows.*

*"This has nothing to do with you, Alexandra," Mom's stern voice. She's driving, eyes glued to the road as the rain starts to fall.*

*"Don't talk to her like that!" Dad, his voice as loud as thunder, startling us both.*

*The car swerves, and I grab for the door handle to steady myself.*

*"Oh, so now you care about her feelings?" she says, eyeing me in the rearview mirror. I must look terrified, because she adds, "Look, you're scaring her."*

*"I'm scaring her? That's rich. You treat her like she doesn't*

*even exist." He accuses.*

*"Yet you're the one who keeps leaving, who keeps tearing this family apart." Mom spits back.*

*"This is about you and me. And how we can't keep doing this." His words are final, a decision made. He won't keep doing this. This time, he won't be coming back.*

*"You can't do this to us. Tell him, Alexandra. Tell him that you don't want him to leave." She pleads, casting me another look in the rearview mirror.*

*"Leave me alone!" I yell, clasping my hands over my ears, burying my head in my lap.*

*That's why I didn't see it. That momentary jerk, the wheel turning slightly to the right as the tires caught in a puddle on the road, hydroplaning.*

*There was no time to react; the car went barreling into the forest.*

"My mother. She lost control of the car. There was no deer, I wasn't driving. I didn't kill my father." My words come out in short bursts of air. I'm hyperventilating.

"No… you didn't," Logan reassures me gently, but I can't look at him, not yet. The guilt unravels itself from around my neck and I can finally breathe. The relief that spreads through me warms me and brings tears to my eyes.

I didn't kill my father. I wasn't even driving. I keep repeating the words in my head, words that I had never thought to put together before, had never thought could be real. It's my new mantra. I have spent these last few months carrying around an unwarranted guilt, trying to make amends. But none of this had anything to do with me, not really.

This changes everything.

# TWENTY

**I SLIP THE PHOTO** into my purse instinctively, sentimentally, and wipe the tears trickling from my eyes.

I think Logan wants to say something, reach out and comfort me, but he keeps his distance. I wouldn't know how to comfort me, either. What do you say to the girl who just found out everything she thought she knew about her life was a lie? That something has messed with her memories. Altered her past. Made her forget the boy she loved and believe she was responsible for killing your own father.

"Ugh!" I let out a guttural cry, my fists slamming against the wall. Pain shoots through my entire arm, but it's no match for the cracks that are already spreading through the rest of me. My entire existence, crumbling before me. I'm on the edge of unraveling completely and will never be able to put myself back together.

"Hey… Lex… breathe, ok? Try and breathe…" Logan's

words find me, but they're muffled, distorted. I'm in my mother's office still, but I'm also somewhere else. Everywhere else. Seeing my entire life flash in front of me. All the forgotten pieces rushing back to me.

I'm having a panic attack. The realization only making me panic more.

I can't breathe.

Logan moves behind me, pulls my body up against his chest so that my back is flat against him. He wraps his arms around me, pulling me in tight, and then starts breathing deeply, slowly. His chest rises, pressing into me so that I can feel his heart beating, feel his steadiness to match against my unsteadiness.

I clench my eyes shut and focus on him. His scent filling my nostrils, his breath warm against my neck. In and out until I'm in a rhythm that matches his. Until I feel calm again. I don't push him away. I choose to let him cradle me for a few moments longer, feeling safe and warm in his arms. The one person who knew me. The real me. And loved me despite it all.

When I finally break away, I know a part of me is missing. Has shriveled up and died. But I ignore the ache. We've wasted too much time and my mother could come back at any minute.

I clear my throat, avoiding Logan's eyes as I reach back into the box at my feet. I stuff some rolled up bills in the pocket of the purse. They were lying on a pile of folded white papers, which I pull out and open. The first page has a formal emblem at the top with the words TrueWood Medical Institute printed in bold.

I quickly scan through the pages, Logan reading over my

shoulder. It's a letter to my mother from a hospital, thanking her for her participation in a rehabilitation program.

"Do you think that's the hospital that they airlifted you to? TrueWood Medical Institute?" Logan pulls out his phone and types in the name. "There's barely any information online about it. No webpage. But there's a Google image."

I take the phone from him and look. It's a massive building, a giant fortress, set back on a property surrounded by trees. There are fences with curled wire at the top squaring it in and bright floodlights screaming down onto a paved lot out front. I recognize it.

"That's where I was. My mother picked me up there with all our stuff before we came here. That's the hospital."

Logan takes the phone back and keeps searching. "I can't find a location, or phone number, or anything."

I flip through the thank you letter again. There's no contact information listed. There isn't even a date, or a name signed to it. I go to toss it back in the box when the words "rehabilitation program" jump back out at me. They make me uneasy.

"What do you think this rehabilitation program is? It can't just be for the accident, can it?" But I already know the answer to that. If it was just rehab after a car accident, there wouldn't be such an air of secrecy around this letter. This Institute.

"We need to find out where this place is. Whatever happened to you to mess up your memories, it has to be linked to this. If we can find it, we can go there and —"

I cut him off. "And what? Break into a secret medical

facility? And do what?"

"I don't know, but they must have files, someone there must know you, know what you've been through."

"We can't raid a facility we know nothing about. We'll be caught and then where will we be? You're right about the files, though. I need to see those files. They must be digitized. They probably have a server or something where they store everything."

I get up and hurry back to my room, grabbing my laptop from my desk. I climb up on my bed, Logan plopping down beside me. Our proximity, a boy sitting on my bed, all of that is lost on me. I'm clouded by so many other thoughts and questions. "Let's see if all those early morning coding classes have paid off." I open my laptop and sign in.

"You learned how to hack into a server in class?" He's bewildered.

"Of course not. I don't have the faintest idea how to do anything besides code a simple website. But there must be something out there, someone has probably leaked something."

I Google "TrueWood Medical Institute," but I don't get any obvious results.

"Try adding memory or conspiracy. There are conspiracies about everything these days," Logan offers and I do. When I hit enter, we have better luck. There aren't any articles feeding us all the answers, but there's a conspiracy website that has a post titled:

TrueWood Memory Project: Fact or Fiction?

I click the link and a short blog post comes up. The same photo that Logan showed me earlier is at the top of the page. It talks about rumors of a secret medical facility in a small town named TrueWood. Describes a world devoid of pain and suffering. A miracle procedure that will erase painful memories and replace them with your biggest hopes and dreams. A "choose your own personality" adventure. Pick your favorite qualities and a state-of-the-art machine will manipulate, overwrite, erase, and reform your mind, your entire identity.

"This can't be real. Do you think this is what happened to you? They changed your memories?" Logan asks and it turns my stomach because it's the best explanation I have.

"If it is what happened to me, I certainly didn't get to choose my own adventure; I didn't have any say in what they did to me."

I feel ill. Violated.

That's my body we're talking about. My brain that someone has been manipulating. Without my permission. Without my knowledge, even.

Who gave them that right?

Logan hesitates. "But would you remember if you did?"

I pause, rolling it around in my head. Is this something I would have voluntarily done? Something to erase my past, erase the accident and give me some peace of mind?

"No, there's no way I would have done that to myself. I thought I killed my father. I've been carrying that guilt around with me for the past six months. I wouldn't have erased bad memories and replaced them with something that awful. And that doesn't seem like the procedure they are talking about here."

I scroll down to the end of the post and there are hundreds of comments. Not surprisingly, the comment section of a conspiracy site is where the Internet comes alive. Most of the commenters are arguing about whether the article is real, with little reasoning behind their opinion other than hope or fear.

> **dug14:** My cuz works for the Institute, man. He told me about it.
> **FakeNewz666**: Bunch of BS. Get a life. lololo
> **SpaceSaviour**: I actually do know someone who works there.
> **Memories4Sale**: Take my memories - $100 each.
> **FakeNewz666**: Yeah, no one wants your pervy thoughts. Lolz.
> **SpaceSaviour:** All the subjects of the trial are kids. I've seen their medical files. I know what really happened to them.
> **Iconost0ne**: I 100% believe this is real. But then, I'm just a crazy conspiracy theorist, ya know...
> **Queenie323**: I hope its reel!
> **SpaceSaviour:** They go to the same private school, connected to TrueWood so the doctors can monitor them.
> **ConspiracyJonez:** This is how it starts. First, they steal your memories, then they implant their own ideas. & microchips. The destruction of others is fine long as it don't effect your own lives.
> **SpaceSaviour:** Srsly guys, this is a big f@*king deal!

Kyle Larson's bullying is anything but good, but thanks to him, the familiar username stands out immediately. SpaceSaviour. I hover over the profile for the user's stats and location. It says they are in their 30s, located in a couple of towns over from Clifton Hills, but I don't believe them. I think they're lying because there's no way that username is a coincidence.

"I think I know who this is." I turn to Logan, wiggling the mouse around SpaceSaviour's avatar. It's a photo of a cartoon warrior with chin length yellowish-brown hair tucked underneath a space helmet. "I'm pretty sure he's the kid everyone picks on in my coding class."

"Great—can you message him on WhatsApp?"

I stare at him blankly. "We aren't friends, I don't know his number."

"Instagram then?"

"He's not exactly the Instagram type," I say as he stares at me. He's about to say something more but freezes in place as the front door downstairs slams shut.

"Alexandra, are you home?" My mother's voice hurries up the stairs. There's an urgency in it, but I can tell she's trying to be calm, hoping to coax a response out of me. I hear her toss her keys on the hallway table and slip off her shoes, heading barefoot into the kitchen. "The headmaster called; said you left school urgently. Are you feeling okay?" Some pots crash together as she fumbles around the kitchen. She's trying to keep her voice steady, a tactic I recognize from when she knows more than she's letting on. She isn't worried about my health; she's worried about what I know.

Our new house isn't the same as our old one. My bedroom window opens to a two-story drop, not a roof that we can climb down. We have to make a run for it. I motion for Logan to follow me as I edge towards the stairs. I may not have lived here that long, but I know the stair's creaks and pops like that of my own body. I take each step slowly, cautiously, and Logan follows my exact footsteps.

We make it to the hallway, and I grab the car keys from the table. They jingle and alert my mother and she darts out of the kitchen.

"Run!" I yell, barreling out the door, Logan's heavy steps behind me.

I jump into the driver's seat and shove the key into the ignition. The engine turns over quickly, and I throw the car into reverse as Logan slams the passenger door closed.

My mother is on the porch, stalled to a stop. She doesn't chase the car, she just watches us, watches me. Her eyes reach mine with an icy glare that freezes my heart. It's not a look I'm used to, but it's something I vaguely remember.

We're down the street driving further and further away from the house when I remember I forgot to close my laptop.

# TWENTY-ONE

**SCOTT JOHNSON AND I** are not friends. But he is the headmaster's son and everyone at the Academy knows where the headmaster lives—their house is one of the largest targets for disgruntled students armed with toilet paper on dark Halloween nights. Or so I'm told.

If SpaceSaviour is Scott Johnson, and he knows about the Institute and their medical trials, I need to know what he knows. Sure, maybe Headmaster Johnson has something to do with all this. It's highly likely that he does. But I need to know what happened to me, and Scott is the quickest path to finding out.

The radio is dialed in to a classic rock station which is playing primarily 90s music. I have my window down and the crisp evening air is refreshing on my face. Clifton Hills isn't a large town, but the Johnson home is some ways outside it, so we have a bit of a drive. Time enough for me to dip back into the well of questions that are threatening to drown me.

"You said there was a funeral? How could there have been a funeral, what did I look like?" I ask, seemingly out of the blue, but it's the one thing I haven't been able to stop thinking about. How could they have my funeral when I was laid up in a hospital bed in a completely different town?

Logan goes rigid, and pales. "You were in a car accident, Lex. It was a closed casket." So, no body, no confirmation that I was, in fact, there. It could have been an empty coffin for all anyone knows.

"Was my mother there?" The question is urgent. It's the key to unlocking everything, I know it is. She couldn't have been there if she was with me. Why would she be at my funeral if she knew I wasn't dead?

"She was there. I didn't see much of her, I was kind of in a state myself," he goes quiet, as if remembering the night. It must kill him to relive it. "Apparently, she made quite a scene. Screaming, slurring her words. Something about it being all your fault, which made no sense since you weren't even driving. Someone escorted her out, and that was the last I heard of her. The last anyone heard of her. She just disappeared. There was a search in case something had happened. But that didn't turn anything up. And then the whole thing just sort of died..."

The word is left lingering. Died. Like I was supposed to have, and yet here I am.

"But she knew I wasn't dead," I whisper, the confusion clogging my mind. "She was at my bedside in the hospital anytime

I opened my eyes. Why would she be at a fake funeral for me when she knew I wasn't dead?"

"Look, Lex. Your mother…" he trails off again, his features twisting as he struggles with his words. "Your mother was… the things she did, how she treated you… maybe this was another one of her games."

My eyes narrow, I have no idea what he's talking about. "How could you even think something like that? She's a complicated woman, I know that. We haven't always gotten along well, especially when it came to you, but that doesn't mean she would do something like fake my funeral. Why would she do that? That doesn't make sense," I say, but Logan shakes his head and dread creeps in because my words feel wrong. There is something tugging at my memory again, something coming loose that's about to unravel another part of me.

"It's more than that, Lex. After our first date, when I walked you to your door, she was waiting for you. As soon as you saw her, your whole attitude changed, as if you retreated into a shell. I had a bad feeling when I left you and I couldn't shake it.

"I tried to find you at school the next morning, but you weren't there. So, I went back to your house that night. I had to make sure you were okay. I climbed up the canopy in your backyard and snuck through your bedroom window." I catch the blush that peeks out above his collar, even though we've already discussed his Dawson's Creek phase. "You were curled up under your comforter. You were so small, so defeated."

*So, who's your friend?*

I hear my mother's voice dripping with venom as clearly as if she were the one sitting next to me, not Logan. She's sprawled against the bottom of the stairs, taking up all the space in the room, blocking my way to the safety of my bedroom.

*Don't fool yourself; you'll never see him again.*

That was her weapon of choice. She'd mock me, pick away at me, try to deflate me anytime I felt whole. It usually sucked the wind from me, knocked the legs out from under me. Clawed through the tape and glue I used to hold myself together.

I remember what people thought about my life back then. How perfect it must have been with my big house, my mother on the town council with an influence over almost anything that happened in our old town. I could do anything I wanted; get into any school that I wanted. I didn't have friends, but I didn't need them; high school was only a blip in a life, none of it mattered. What mattered was who you were when you made it out the other side. But just because I had a big house and a perfect yard didn't mean there wasn't something rotting inside it.

Logan was the first person I ever told about her. The first time I had ever said the words aloud. The first time anyone had cared enough to ask.

Our conversation circles through my mind. A merry-go-round, each truth a different wooden horse moving faster and faster until all I see are giant white teeth and glaring dead eyes.

*"Do you ever just feel... so tired?"*

*"It's the mind games, the way she undermines everything I say, everything I do."*

*"It eats at you, slowly, you don't even notice it at first, but there comes a point where you realize that it's eaten away everything that makes you, you."*

*"You can't break away. You can't just leave, not when you're a sixteen-year-old girl in a small town in the middle of nowhere. Not when you have no friends, because your mother keeps running them off."*

*"I have one more year I have to make it through, one more year until I'm free."*

*"All I want is to be free."*

Tears didn't fall anymore at that point. They dried up long before, leaving a deep emptiness, a loneliness, a bone-aching tiredness that I dragged with me everywhere I went.

That familiar emptiness carves its old home in me now, making me hollow as the memories ooze back in. Thick and sticky. A sickening tar filling up all the old empty holes that I had forgotten were there.

I veer the car off the road onto the shoulder, a little chaotically. I can't breathe. I can't see. My hands are a shield against my head, but memories start flooding in and I can't stop them. My childhood, my *real* childhood, was mind games and manipulation. I can't believe… But I can. I can believe it because I can remember it now. The way she would press down on me, making me small. Convincing me that I wasn't worth it.

*I am seven, and all I want is a treehouse. I saved all my money to buy a build-your-own kit. We had the perfect cluster of trees that were asking to be the foundation for it. The morning of the delivery, there were noises from the backyard. That's when I discovered she hired a crew to cut down the trees to build a pool.*

*I am fourteen, my first year of high school, that precious time when everyone is new and trying to fit in and make an impression. I fell in with a group of girls who lived on my street. I was blissfully smitten with them, having never been one of the popular girls before. But then they turned on me, one by one. Accusing me of talking to each other behind another's back, spreading rumors and making up stories. They showed me printouts of emails from my account with words I had never written, never even thought before. My mother's words, camouflaged behind my screen name. Shredding through my friendships. Ruining my reputation so I had nowhere else to be but home.*

"My mother, she was..." I want to call her all the names that are as sharp as the pain cutting through my chest, but my voice cracks. I have to stop because all those lost tears have found me again and are threatening to flood the car.

I rip in two, nothing but jagged edges and bruised surfaces. A rotting piece of fruit that reveals itself after the magic glimmer has worn off. Sour to the taste, pungent with lies.

A quiet sob slips out and I bring my hands to my mouth to shove it back in. Logan's fingers find my chin first and gently tilts my head up. He's inches from my face, running his fingers over my features, down my cheeks, across my eyebrows. Making sure I'm whole. Convincing himself that I'm real. There's such intimacy, such familiarity, and it makes me nervous.

I pull away, my head spinning with a rush of memories flooding back in. Good ones, bad ones, confusing ones. I don't know what to do with them. One life vs. another. These old memories vs. my new ones. I don't know who I am anymore, so I take everything, all these memories, and shove them back inside, burying them deep.

Everything is so quiet, but my mind, my body, is anything but silent. Logan's beside me, an electricity jumping from his body to mine. Every so often, his hand brushes up against mine and lightning strikes up my arm.

I've found a little piece of myself again. But there's a heavy sadness that comes with it because he's a stranger to me. This me, the me I am now. The girl who killed her father, who was shipped away to a reform school, who hasn't had her first kiss.

How do I make these two girls one? How do I pick and choose what parts of me define me? How do I unravel everything that has happened to me, to get me to this point? And what the hell am I supposed to do with this new version of myself?

# TWENTY-TWO

**THE BEST WAY TO** get over an emotional breakdown about your terrible mother and the lost memories you didn't know you had, in front of the boy you used to know and love, is to shove it back down inside and keep moving. Right?

We've been driving twenty minutes, both pretending I'm not just a puddle in a driver's seat, before we spot Scott Johnson's big Victorian house. It's a corner lot with many vantage points for toilet paper warfare, but also little cover for a stealthy approach.

Mr. Johnson's SUV isn't in the driveway, thankfully. Though if my mother just got home from meeting with him, he can't be too far behind. Logan follows me to the door, and we wait as the doorbell echoes through the emptiness of the first floor. It's mostly window and I can see into the front hallway. Pristine hardwood floors, jackets hung up neatly, a few pairs of shoes standing at attention. There's not even a shoelace out of place.

There's a sticker on the door saying the premises is protected by an alarm system, a blinking light of a camera mounted under the awning. I try to square my body to avoid it, but there's no way I won't be recognized if anyone watches it back.

There's no movement to answer. School let out a while ago— Scott has to be here by now. I ring the bell again, and then again. Finally, footsteps dredge along the floor in our direction. Through the window, Scott comes into view and pauses, catching sight of us standing on his doorstep. I am almost certain he's considering leaving us there. Turning around and pretending he isn't home.

But then his shoulders relax a little and he comes to unlock the door.

"Hi Scott!" I start, the light familiarity in my voice sounding fake as it leaves my mouth. I'm not sure I've ever even spoken to him before.

"Alexandra..." he says, but his eyes are on Logan, not me. "What's up?"

"I, well, we, were wondering if maybe... can we come in?"

"That depends. Who's your friend?"

*Who's your friend?*

I shake my mother's words aside and try to focus. Scott must have heard about what happened at school. About the boy who was yelling about me being dead, whom security was quick to drag away. If he takes that story at face value, then I'm trying to get him to invite me and some lunatic into his home. But if he knows more than he's letting on, maybe he will be more willing to speak to us. Maybe I won't sound like the lunatic if I tell him the truth.

"This is Logan. I knew him before I moved here, but he thought I was dead, and I don't remember him. Or didn't remember him until he showed up at school this morning. Something is going on with me, and I think you can help."

Was that only this morning? So many years, so many memories coming back to me at once. I have lived a whole other lifetime in this one afternoon.

Scott is eying us both suspiciously, curiously. His mind ticking, trying to figure out if he can trust what we're saying. Wondering what other doors he will open if he opens this one for us.

"Did Hannah send you?"

"What does Hannah have to do with this?" I ask and a blush works its way across Scott's face. He must have a crush on her.

"I can't help you." He says evenly, trying to end the conversation. But I have no other leads; this conversation can't end. I resort to begging.

"Please Scott, I need answers, and I don't know where else to go."

"Why would I have information like that?" He hesitates, but his eyes light up a little, betraying him. They are eager, like he can't wait to tell someone other than strangers on the Internet what he knows. But there's a hint of something else there too, something more like fear.

"You write those stories, for the Internet? Under the name SpaceSaviour? And well, we came across a forum with that username. He sounded like he knew what he was talking about, about this conspiracy...." I pause and lean in a little like we ourselves are conspiring. "I thought I killed my father. These last few months I have hated myself for what I did. It's been a living hell, but it's not true. The accident, my memories, they aren't real. How is that possible? How have I forgotten my entire life? I need to know and I'm fairly sure you can tell me."

"Maybe I can, but if they find out I told you—"

"I won't tell anyone, I promise. I just need to know what's wrong with me."

Scott doesn't seem to need much more time to contemplate; he pushes the door open with his foot. Logan grabs it and we let ourselves in.

Scott brings us through the house to a door nestled under the giant staircase leading up. There's a sign on it reading PRIVATE in big red letters, but he opens it to another set of stairs that lead down. There's a light dangling from the ceiling, casting an eerie glow as we follow him down the narrow steps into the basement.

The bottom of the staircase opens into a cement room. It's cold, both figuratively and literally, and it smells like an old pair of shoes. There's little to no furniture except for a giant desk. More command station than workspace, and a large bookshelf overflowing with comic books.

The walls are covered in brightly colored posters for school events and parties that have happened in the town over the last few months. Maybe even years. I have never seen Scott at a school function, let alone a house party, but clearly, that isn't because he didn't know about them.

He goes to a small closet on the other side of his command center and pulls out two folding lawn chairs. He sets them up in front of us before sitting down in an over-sized computer chair. I'm pretty sure that thing belong in the cockpit of a fighter jet, not some teenager's basement.

"So, how can I help?" he asks, sitting in his chair. It's his throne and this is his fortress. Any hesitation he had was left at the door because now he has a captive audience, and he has the information that we need. He is the one in power, a position I imagine he isn't entirely used to.

"Like I said… I think something happened to me. To my memory? Logan told me about my life before I came to the Academy. It's different than what I remember…" I pause, hoping Scott will catch my drift, but he remains infuriatingly stoic. I'm going to have to spell it out for him. "The person who posted on the forum said they'd seen medical files. That the subjects of the trial were students that went to a private school. I need to know if you remember anything from the files you saw. Anything that might help me figure out what happened to me."

He lets me hang for a moment longer, but then his shoulders relax as he gives in. "I can do you one better than telling you what I remember." He fights to hide a smile as he spins around in his chair and wakes up his computer. There are multiple giant screens mounted to the desk and they all come to life at once.

He pulls up File Explorer and navigates to a folder called homework. This reveals a few files with assignment names, different dates. I'm about to call him out on his bullshit. I need more than school assignments. But then he changes the folder properties to display hidden items and more files appear. Many more files.

"What do you want to know?" He opens various documents. Record files. No, patient files. Medical forms, photos of people, a few newspaper articles. Window after window of different case studies and profiles, all with the Institute's logo at the top. A chill runs through my spine.

"How did you get these?" I ask, my voice cracking. Scott seems proud of his bounty, his hidden treasure. His coyness has turned into something closer to bragging now.

"Whatever this Institute is, my dad is part of it. The Academy is part of it. I've seen him at his laptop, being all sketchy. Obviously, I wanted to know what he was hiding. I thought it was porn." I grimace, and Scott quickly continues. "I hacked his computer from our home network. He has access to an encrypted EMR system. I couldn't bypass the encryption, but my dad has his login set to remember the password. With one little click, I had access to all the files for the students at the Academy."

"All the students?" Logan asks and Scott nods.

"From what I can tell, yes."

"Show me my file," I demand, the words tumbling out urgently so I can't take them back.

Scott is already closing all the windows and searching through the file names. I see it the same time he does. My heart races as he opens it and for a minute, I wonder if I should take it back. I want to know; I want answers, but I'm scared of what they will be. But it's too late, there is no going back. The documents pop up with medical files, newspaper clippings, photographs.

Shaw, Alexandra
Reason for admission: Careless driving that
led to the death of her father

No surprises there. Except for the fact that I wasn't driving.

That I didn't kill my father. Apparently.

My stomach lurches as I stare at the images. The first one is my grade eleven school photo. The year I met Logan. The year of the accident. I look content. Neither happy nor sad. But completely unaware of what my future holds.

The second photo makes my hands tremble. It's me, sprawled on a metal operating table, arms and legs secured by leather straps. There are screens behind me with lines, charts, and graphs. On the table beside me is a metal tray with large tools that belong in a dentist's office, only bigger.

The most disturbing part, though, the part that makes me hold my breath, is the noticeable contusion above my right eyebrow. There's a small, rectangular piece of plastic sticking out of it with a wire running to the rack of computers behind me.

I leave my body, my anxiety pushing me right out of my skin. Seeing myself sprawled vulnerably on a table, is one thing. To think—no, to know—that this happened to me...

"What the hell," Logan mumbles, breaking my trance, and I let the breath I've been holding come roaring out in a heavy sigh. But I can't tear away from the photo; I can't process what I'm seeing.

"Pretty wild, right?" Scott says, as if this is a cool story arc in a sci-fi movie. Not my life. Not his life. Not all these student's lives.

"What's that thing in her head? What are they doing to her?" Logan's voice comes out tight, a mix of anger and fear.

"Think of it like a webpage." Scott is nodding at me, referring to our coding class, but there's no way what he's saying is going to make sense to me. My brain can't move past that image. Past the reality of what happened to me. "Download an image, correct it in a photo editor and then save it with the same name. When it's uploaded back to the website, the new image replaces the old one. The file is overwritten. Pretend the website is her brain."

"That's what you think they're doing with her memories?"

"That's what I know they're doing with her memories. With everyone's memories." Scott is defiant, but his smile falters at Logan's accusing expression.

"Even yours?"

"That's none of your business." Scott's jaw clenches and the eager, helpful savior slowly slips away, replaced by something more distant.

"But you've read through everyone else's files—their personal files—like *that* is somehow *your* business?" Logan moves closer and gets right up in Scott's face. They knock into each other's shoulders, start pushing back and forth a little. This snaps me out of whatever zone I was lost in.

I put my hand on his shoulder, and he eases slightly. He has a point, though. "It does seem convenient that you are totally aware of what is going on and you have all these files." Scott is quiet, but I glare at him until he caves.

"Look, all I know is that there's something not entirely right yet. The procedure, the uploads if you will, they are supposed to overwrite the memory, replace it. But it doesn't always stick. There are triggers. Things that make the original memory resurface. Running into someone from your past who isn't part of your new memories, for example." Scott eyes Logan to emphasize his point. "Or reading a book that makes you think differently. When you start to question things, or your mind gets confused about what's real, the new memory can start to slip. And the more it slips, the more the original memories come back."

"So what, you have all your original memories then?" When he nods, the other questions continue to flow. "And they let you keep them? I can't see how that is good for business." He lets out another sigh.

"They don't, usually. When this happens, they usually send people back to be factory reset. It's not unusual for someone to be reset multiple times. It's a quicker process, since all the mappings are already in place. Though to be honest, I don't think it works any better than the first time around."

Multiple resets. If what Scott is saying is true, it's possible I've been reset before. Multiple times. And each time, I'm somehow triggered and find my way back.

"Surely a huge medical institution who can conduct these kinds of widespread experiments would have better control over their process," I say, more to myself than anyone else.

Scott keeps opening files. Faces of my classmates stare back at me. One piled on top of the other. As he scrolls, their identities fade until they aren't even people anymore, just head counts, numbers in a filing system. I catch glimpses of their medical records. Alarming details about their lives. Words piling on words, lives upon lives that led everyone right here. Just like me.

Though most of them have absolutely no idea that something is going on.

I gasp when he gets to the two most familiar faces in the school. Kayla and Hannah. Of course, if this affects everyone here, it affects them too. But until I saw their faces, I somehow hoped it wouldn't be true.

I can't help myself; I lean in closer to read the small print of their files.

Porter, Kayla
Reason for admission: Promiscuity leading to near-death
complications during teenage pregnancy

Collins, Hannah
Reason for admission: Restrictive eating, self-harm

My stomach churns. I'm going to vomit. In this day and age, admitting someone to a reform school for these kinds of struggles is sickening. I know nothing of their past, their family, where they came from. But I never considered what their story would be. Never considered that they would be here for something so oppressing.

What kind of school is this? Who would do this to their children? Why do none of us have any memory of what happened before?

Whatever is going on, it's happening to all the students. All my friends. This isn't just about me anymore.

# TWENTY-THREE

**THE ACADEMY OF THE** undead.

But of course, we aren't dead. We're all very much alive. With different memories, but alive.

"I still don't get it, why would a parent put their child through something like this? What do they get in return? It's such a risk?" As horrifying as these files are, it still doesn't answer the big questions.

Scott squints his eyes closed and pulls at his hair as if he's fighting some inner battle and losing. "I read everyone's files, okay? You win—" He glares at Logan but softens when his eyes return to me. "You've heard the rumors at school, about what kids did before they came here? Drugs, guns, self-harm. These kids, every single one of them other than myself, had something terrible happen to them that almost killed them. Accidents, attempted murders, overdoses. Some tried to take their own lives…"

Scott stares at me, as if this should answer everything. It takes me a minute, but then it does. It all makes sense. The days after the accident, my mother at my bedside. I know those memories aren't real, but there is a realness to them. Parents grieving at their child's bedside, praying for a miracle that will give them their child back. Easy prey.

"Most parents would do anything. Sign their kid up for anything, if it meant they would live to see another day. And if they could take it a step further and change the memories, emotions, and feelings that led to their child's end. If they could erase the bad memories and replace them with something good..."

Scott taps the side of his nose with one finger. Bingo.

I'm sick with the idea. Who wouldn't rather erase the bad parts of their life and replace it with something good instead of live with it, deal with it, heal from it? Wouldn't every parent love the opportunity to fix their troubled child? Change their urges, habits, and personalities? A quick, easy fix.

But it's not quick, and it's not easy and clearly, it's not without its faults, if I'm standing here with my memory intact.

"If that's true though, what about Lex? The accident was her mother's fault, she wasn't getting into trouble, so why the fake memories, why the reform school?"

Scott shrugs, and my stomach sinks. I try to think back to the night of the accident, my entire childhood. Why would my mother want to erase everything, unless it was for her own sake? Maybe none of this is about me at all, but about saving her ass, making me forget about what kind of person she actually is.

Scott moves the mouse back to a document file. He hits a quick CTRL-P on the keyboard, and a printer whirls to life beside us. The first page off is a newspaper article. The headline speaks of a rainstorm, a car accident, a mother's tragic loss. It reiterates mostly what Logan has already told me. A young girl, Alexandra Holland, brought to the hospital, air lifted elsewhere and then pronounced dead.

The next article is larger, and instead of a picture of me, there is one of my mother. I pull it off the printer tray to read it more carefully. This one tells the story of a grieving mother burdened by guilt after she loses control of her car and kills her only child. That mother tries to bury her guilt in the bottom of bottles, causes a scene at her daughter's funeral.

Then came the whispered accusations. Just rumors at first. Students telling of passive aggressive threats to stay away from her daughter. Teachers who had noticed trouble at home. There's a quote from a teacher expressing her concern and even going as far as to ask whether this was really an accident.

I slam the paper down on the desk, the lines of text starting to blur. I can't tell if it's my eyesight acting up again or if there are tears clouding my vision. I don't know what I feel.

My first instinct, despite everything, is a longing for my mother. A knowing pain of what reading those words about her must have done to her.

Then there's a sense of relief. My story, my secret, people noticed. People saw how she was and what she was doing. But then the anger sets in. People saw, people knew, but no one did anything. No one stood by me, except Logan.

The medical documents are rolling off the printer next. There are so many pages. I'm grabbing them up one by one, resisting the urge to read them until I have them all in my hands. "All of this is… messed up in its own right, but the thing I don't get, why make me think I killed my father?" The question has been swirling around in my head. It doesn't seem to fit with what they claim to be doing. If they are changing people's personalities for the better, to make them happier and more productive, why cripple someone with guilt and fabricated pain?

Before anyone can offer their thoughts, the front door slams closed above us and Scott jumps in his chair. There are heavy footsteps, but also the *click-click-click* of high heels. Mr. Johnson is home, and he's not alone.

I grab the rest of the papers from the printer, fold them in half, and scribble my name across the front of it. I stuff it into a comic on Scott's bookshelf, hoping whoever is upstairs won't go as far as searching his room. Logan is on his feet, but we're two frightened animals with nowhere to go. I glance around the concrete basement for windows or doors, and there is nothing. The windows that exist are way too high to easily climb through.

The footsteps get louder and louder, moving back through the house until there's a loud *bang, bang* on the door at the top of the stairs.

"Scott, are you down there?" Headmaster Johnson's voice carries down the stairway, settling into my ears, urging me to run, to escape, but I can't.

The door at the top of the stairs opens and Scott freezes, gaping at me as I look to Logan. I don't know what to do.

"I'll go see what he wants," Scott whispers, though that can't be our best plan, our only plan. But there's nothing to do but watch as he climbs the stairs and closes the door behind him.

Logan grabs my hand. It's a firm grasp, but reassuring. My heart rate slows a little, my nerves settle. I turn to him, to tell him what I feel, to put it into words. But the door opens again and there are feet on the top step, the step below that, the step below that. They aren't the feet of a high school boy; they are a pair of dainty heels with red soles tap-tap-tapping down the steps.

They reach the bottom of the staircase, and we have nowhere to hide.

I'm still searching for a way to escape when my eyes settle on the woman standing at the bottom of the stairs. She's wearing a dark blouse tucked into a pencil skirt and her hands are on her waist, authoritatively.

On the steps above her are a pair of heavily booted feet that reach up to black pants before being cut off by the ceiling. I don't need an active imagination to fill in the blanks of who could be waiting at the top of the stairs, blocking our only exit.

"Miss Shaw. My name is Dr. Anderson. I think we should talk." She saunters towards Scott's command center and sits in his captain's chair, motioning us to the empty lawn chairs. "Won't you please have a seat?"

"My mother called you, didn't she?" I don't move. Dr. Anderson nods in response.

"Your mother only wants what is best for you. She's worried about you."

I roll my eyes. "She's not worried about me. She's worried that somehow this is going to reflect badly on her. Who are you? How do you even know her?" I'm sure I already know the answer, but I want to hear it from her. I want her to confirm everything Scott has shown me is true.

Dr. Anderson glances towards the computer, but the screens are dark. "What do you already know?"

"Know about what?" I try, but her expression says she doesn't believe me for a second. "Oh, you mean about how you people prey on kids who have almost died? How you pretend you are helping, say you are going to make them better, but instead you erase all their memories and turn them into shallow replicas of who they are?"

"Who they were, Miss Shaw. But no, we don't prey on anybody. We present opportunities. We offer lifelines that people are often desperately seeking in those dark, tragic moments. The choice is entirely up to them."

I scoff. "What choice? You put something like that on the table in front of someone at risk of losing their child. What other choice do they have? You're manipulating the situation, taking advantage of people at their lowest when they are likely to do anything to change the situation."

"That's a dismal way of putting it. We gave you a second chance at life. We moved you and your mother to a new town away from the rumors and history that were clearly tearing your mother apart. We repaired your relationship, gave you new friends, a new chance to live up to your potential. Are you telling me you aren't happy with your new life?"

"You erased everything that I was. Everything that made me who I was. You made me think I killed my father!" The word father seems to echo through the cement basement. Dr. Anderson says nothing, but something changes in her expression. She isn't as confident as she was moments ago. "Did my mother know what you were going to do to me? That you were going to poke around in my head, erase everything I knew and reprogram me?"

"Your mother knew everything, Alexandra. She had full control of how your memories were restyled and uploaded back into your memory bank. We work with the parents to create a calmer, happier, and more productive future."

"And my father, was that your idea or hers?"

There's a long pause where she seems to struggle to find an answer. "We were trying something new with that. I'm not sure it was our best work."

My mother knew. She did this intentionally. Of course, she did. Logan draws a breath in deeply, trying to soothe himself. I try to match his breathing. Not only was I part of an experimental trial, but I was an experiment within the experiment that turned out not to be their best work.

"Why would she do that, though? It doesn't make sense," I say more to myself than anyone else, but Dr. Anderson answers me anyway.

"That's something you would have to ask her." As if, it were that easy. Dr. Anderson's tone is stern, clear that she will not give me anything else, so I try another angle.

"So, then what, we are shipped off to the robot farm for you to continue to study?"

"It's hardly a farm, and you are hardly a robot, Miss Shaw. You are painting us like heartless monsters. We genuinely want to help you, help your family. The process is cautious, it's not rushed. We keep you under observation to make sure there are no issues with the overwriting, and when you are stable, we relocate you to your new life. It's a rather seamless transition for most."

"And those who do not have a seamless transition?" Logan chimes in and I remember the room they held him in, the basement with all the dark cells and student files. Deceased student files.

"They go wild," I whisper. Dr. Anderson pinches her nose with her perfectly manicured fingers and I'm not sure if she's going to continue. If she's going to admit to these deaths, but she clears her throat and goes on.

"Yes, well, there have been some instances where the overwriting does not completely take hold. Unfortunately, it creates a level of deep confusion that, in some cases, has led to some extreme consequences."

"And what, everyone there is a ticking time bomb waiting to go off? Do you even know who is stable and who isn't? Could this happen to anyone? Everyone?" Logan is getting heated in his accusations. "Lex, they stole your memories and replaced them. They erased me from your life entirely! This is not okay!"

Dr. Anderson closes her eyes, taking deep breath to manage

her patience. "As hard as it may be to hear, Mr. Owens, none of this is about you. In fact, without you, Alexandra wouldn't be in the situation she is currently in. I didn't want to have to go to the extreme, but you are giving me no choice."

At that, the booted feet waiting on the stairs descend, followed by two more, and two guards come into full view. There are guns at their hips and batons in their hands and penetrating eyes that make my body tense, readying itself to run. But we still have nowhere to go.

"Woah, okay, hold on." I put my hands up in surrender. I'm on my feet, but they're heavy cement blocks. The basement is a vast emptiness, but anywhere I go, I'll still be within someone's reach. My heart pounds in my ears. So loud, I can't focus. "Dr. Anderson, please call off your dogs." I beg her for help, but there's a sadness in her eyes, and I realize we're on our own.

The guards are waiting for Dr. Anderson's direction, and she gives a subtle nod. As they approach, Logan and I both desperately try to flee, but it's useless. Their grip tightens on our arms, and they start pulling us towards the stairs.

"Please, Dr. Anderson, you don't need to do this."

"I'm sorry, Alexandra. You had to know that we couldn't let you leave here with this information. It's too delicate. Who knows what it would do if you told anyone at the Academy? It's for the safety of your friends, and of yourself. I wish there were another way. But I promise you, you won't remember any of this. Everything will go back to how it was."

The guards force us up the stairs and through the house.

There's no sign of Headmaster Johnson or Scott anywhere. No one I can call to for help. I'm lashing against the guard's chest, trying to break free, but I'm held too tightly. They're going to erase a part of my head again, and there is nothing I can do about it.

Logan is dragged behind me. I try to crane my neck to see him. Catch one last look of him before they make me forget him completely, but I can't see past the black chest holding me.

"Logan!" I yell. I am outside now, being dragged towards a white van. "Logan!"

And then I hear him, he's moving in another direction away from me, but I hear him.

"Don't forget me Lex, please don't forget me!"

It's the last thing I hear.

# TWENTY-FOUR

**I OPEN MY EYES** Monday morning, and everything is, like, blurry. My head pounds and my mouth is like sand and O-M-G, my entire body screams at me when I move. Ow, ow, ow. But my mind is clear and for the first time in, like, months, I feel like me.

Me: Seventeen. Favorite color: Pink. Favorite Singer: Taylor Swift. Favorite Book: *Little Women*.

Also me: Killer of father. Redeeming my future. Making my mom proud.

I need to get out of the oversized t-shirt I slept in and find something proper to wear. Something my size, which isn't this ratty. I should toss it, but it has *The Strokes* fading across the front. I'd hate to throw out something that supports a charity organization… I think?

My closet is a mess, and I stare at it dumbfounded. This is not me. I am not a mess. It's as though someone rifled through my clothing, pulling things off hangers in a hurry. I take a quick inventory; nothing seems to be missing. School uniforms freshly pressed. Weekend clothes in all my favorite bright colors hanging at the ready. My Mary Janes all nicely lined up in a row. But something feels off. A little out of place.

I rub the sleep from my eyes and habitually grab for a crisp white blouse and my uniform skirt. I pull them on snuggly, admiring myself in the floor length mirror. I look like I do every morning. Carefully coiffed hair, just covering the scar from the accident above my right eyebrow. A bright morning glow. A perfectly average seventeen-year-old. I study myself a moment longer, my lips pulled tight in a judgmental tilt.

I reach for my phone, usually on my bedside table, but it isn't there. I grab my messenger bag, but there's only books and pens taking up the inside space. If I lost it again, Mom is going to kill me. But we aren't allowed to bring phones into the classrooms, I probably just forgot it in my locker.

Mom is in the kitchen when I make my way downstairs, happily humming to herself, and cooking something for breakfast. The concerned expression she wears as I walk in quickly shifts to a smile, something I mirror.

"Good morning! That smells amaaaaaahzing." I sit at the table. Mom is working at the butcher-block island, up early yet again to make me breakfast, to see me off to school. Despite the accident, despite killing my father, she greets me every morning with love and a warm meal.

"Good morning darling. You look bright and chipper this

morning," she offers, placing a plate in front of me. My stomach grumbles right on time.

"I slept well last night. I feel rested." I realize it's the first time in a while that these words are true. My sleep has been fitful and restless, full of strange dreams, though I can't quite remember what about.

"I'm happy to hear that. You've been… not quite yourself lately. I'm relieved to see that you're finding your way back." Mom looks at me a beat too long and I'm flushed with insecurity.

What does she really see when she looks at me? How much more can I do to make everything up to her, to prove to her that I'm trying, I'm doing my best. That I am the daughter she always thought I was, and everything that happened is in the past?

I take a bite of toast, the peanut butter settling onto my tongue in a thick coat. I'm overcome with gratitude for Mom, for my new life, for this second chance. How many kids get the opportunity to rebuild themselves?

I pick up my bag and head to the front door, ready to leave for school, but something stops me. A tugging, pulling me back to the kitchen.

"I love you Mom, you know that, right?" I ask, my mouth still sticky with peanut butter.

"Honey, of course. I love you too. So much. You have no idea," she returns a look that's soft and genuine and my heart floods.

We're going to be okay.

The morning sun warms my face as I make my way to school.

I swear I haven't seen my friends in weeks. Though it was just a few days ago, we were sharing beers at Brian's party. I'm stoked to see them waiting for me as they always do when I approach the front gate.

"Good morning!" I call cheerfully as I approach.

Kim is standing with Kyle, the two of them having a tense conversation. I'm not sure if they're *together,* together, but they have been the best of friends since coming here, apparently. Something that stretches beyond friendship, whether it's romantic or not.

You'd think that would make me a third wheel, but it doesn't. We've been friends ever since my first day here. I clumsily dropped all my books at my locker and Kyle stopped to help me pick them up, later introducing me to Kim. Seeing them waiting for me at the gates as they do every morning warms me.

"And a good morning to you!" Kyle returns cheerily, relieved to be able to pull his attention from whatever spat he and Kim were having.

But she seems less enthused at my interruption. Her eyes narrow, scanning me from head to toe with an air of judgment.

"You alright Kim?" I ask, confused by her cold shoulder. "How was the rest of your weekend?"

"Fine…" she trails off, as if giving me more information about it arms me against her somehow.

I give her an uncertain look, but I'm not going to let my surly friend ruin my good mood today, so I let it go.

There are a few other students lingering around the gate, not quite ready to take the steps into school to start yet another week. Hannah Collins is leaning against the stone wall. Her cardigan pulled down over her hands, her eyes darting around in a panic.

I imagine she's looking for Kayla Porter. Hannah is basically attached to Kayla's hip, her own personal flotation device in this rocky, turbulent high school sea. But that's the cost of popularity. You can cling to the Queen Bee, but you're also in debt to her status. She can take you or leave you at will. My heart clenches momentarily, imagining how Hannah must feel if Kayla abandoned her at the gate and left her to fend for herself.

"Shall we, ladies?" Kyle asks, making a show of lifting his elbows into wings, offering one to each of us. I immediately take his arm, struck by how grateful I am to have such true and loyal friends. Friends who won't just leave me if something better comes along. Kim grabs his other arm, a little more hesitantly, but I can tell that whatever she is mad at him about is starting to fade.

We skip past the gate, my friends completely oblivious to everyone else. But I feel like I'm being watched. I look around self-consciously and spot Hannah eyeing us as we pass her expression one of worry and suspicion. When I look away, I can tell her stare is still boring into my back, studying my movements.

It sends a shudder through me, but I keep walking.

The hallway is crowded, but I try to greet everyone as usual. A perky smile, a waved hello. These are my peers, the people I am growing with, learning from, connecting with. But the hallway is stuffier than usual; people seem to bump into me, staring at me like I interrupted them talking about me.

"Did… something happen? Am I missing something?" I ask Kim, but she shrugs, slamming her locker shut and adjusting her bag on her shoulders. Her perma-grin wavers a touch and it does little to settle my thoughts.

Usually when kids act like this after the weekend, it's because someone got drunk at a party and did something stupid. But nothing out of the ordinary happened at Brian's party Friday night. Kim, Kyle and I took our usual spots along the wall, observing our peers, too afraid to mingle with them. Kayla was there with that college boy she's been seeing on and off, Hannah at their heels as always. There was drinking, dancing, a few younger girls in tears. But nothing big happened. Nothing that should put everyone on edge. Definitely not anything that would make them stare at me. So why is everyone staring at me?

I'm thankful that Kyle and I have programming class first. At least I'm not left on my own. We take our usual seat behind our computers, but I can't focus on today's coding lesson. I swear, anytime I look up, someone is staring at me. Whispering about me.

"Kyle, have you heard anything? About me? People keep staring at me," I whisper, running my eyes across the room, heads turning any time I land on them. All of them except for Headmaster Johnson's son, Scott. We've never spoken before, but he's the only student not chicken enough to hold my gaze.

"I think… well you should probably talk to Kim about it? Not me," Kyle offers, unhelpfully.

"If you know something and aren't telling me, Kyle, I'm

going to punch you," I respond, which makes him bristle.

He smirks and I want to slap it right off his face. "Well, they're just waiting for the show." He leans back in his chair, crossing his arms over his chest. I stare at him blankly, waiting for him to continue. "Have you seen Kayla yet today?"

A bolt of dread zig zags down my back at the mention of Kayla. She's not exactly someone I socialize with, either. We are on completely different planes of existence in this school and Kyle putting her name in the same sentence as mine must be a trick.

"What about Kayla?" I whisper, trying to make the pieces fit.

"Word has it, she's on a hot rampage looking for you. After what you did at the party last Friday." He studies me, waiting for the light bulb to flick on above my head but nothing happens. I still have no idea what he's talking about.

"You're going to have to give me more than that. Nothing happened Friday night," I nudge, but the blood is rushing through my ears and I'm not even sure I will hear him when he answers.

"Her boyfriend—or whatever he is—that college guy? Everyone saw you swapping spit with him in the backyard. Kayla's out for blood."

"Wait, what? No, that's… no, there is no way that happened." But as I'm saying the words, my mind is reeling, desperately trying to think back to everything that happened that night. I was drinking, sure. But there's no way I drank enough to make out with a college boy I don't even know. Especially not the boyfriend of the most popular girl in school. "There is no way." I try again. But it doesn't help convince me of anything.

I squeeze my eyes shut, bringing myself back to the party. The loud music. People everywhere. And there is a boy. Brawny arms, a woodsy smell. Reaching for me. A tether pulling from my gut.

I snap my eyes back open. No. I would remember making out with someone at a party.

"I… I have to go," I mumble, grabbing for my books and standing up so abruptly that my chair falls to the ground. Mr. Morrison barely raises an eyebrow as I bolt from the room.

# TWENTY-FIVE

**I DON'T KNOW WHERE** I'm going. I need to find someone who can help me make sense of this. But with a pit in my stomach, I realize I don't know who that is.

I wander through the empty hallway. The lights are too bright, and I strain to find my way. There are flashes every time I close my eyes. Me, pressed up against a boy. Strong arms, reaching for me. A familiar scent filling my nose.

I want to scream.

This can't be real, because there's no way I would have made out with some college boy at a party, especially not when he's linked to Kayla. I know better than to mess with the Queen Bee.

Kim has spare while I have programming, which means she'll be in the Yearbook room doing extra work. Even though she's being a crap friend right now, I don't know who else to ask for help. I slink through the empty hallways, jumping at every sound in the distance.

I worry that Kayla is going to appear and challenge me to a duel right in the middle of the school. For a split second, I wonder if I'd win. Then shake my head at how ridiculous all of this even is.

I push through the half-open door to the classroom. I figured Kim would be alone, but there are a few other students making up time and they all look up at me.

Ms. Walker is standing at the front of the room, watching me. I expect her to ask what I'm doing here or tell me to go back to class, but she just waits to see what I will do. I give her a small smile and then join Kim at her workstation.

"Hey," she says, not looking up from her computer screen. "What's up?" Ugh, her flippancy is grating. Here I am, running through the school like a maniac trying to figure out why everyone thinks something happened that didn't. Meanwhile, Kim is just happily sitting in class arranging photos into templates for a stupid book of faces no one is ever going to look at again.

"What happened at the party Friday? With Kayla's boyfriend?" The edge to my voice at least makes her look up from her computer.

"I told you; I don't know what you're talking about." She's pretending to be bored of the conversation, but it's just a way to avoid meeting my stare.

"OMG, you're obvs lying! You're supposed to be my friend, why won't you just tell me?" I raise my voice louder than I mean to and catch the attention of the other people in the class. I expect

Ms. Walker to kick me out, since I don't belong here in the first place. But she's reading at the front of the class, completely ignoring us.

"Why won't I tell you? Well, we aren't exactly friends, are we?" Kim's response is a punch to the gut. We've been friends ever since I started going here. We've had sleepovers and mall trips and confided in each other about crushes and secrets. If that isn't a friend, I don't know what is.

"How can you say that?" The hurt is obvious in my voice, but instead of calming her, it seems to ignite her.

"Just because you and Kayla got into some fight and you lost your status as miss popular, you think everyone is just begging to take Kayla's place? We've hardly spoken since you started here and all of a sudden, we're besties?" Kim's voice wavers slightly and I can tell she's not used to speaking her mind when it's not a prepared speech in front of a school.

"What are you talking about? We are besties. Since I started here. You, me and Kyle. Best friends forever." I say, though the words feel wrong on my tongue. A little cheesy and cliche. The panic starts to swell in my chest. A pressure behind my eyes.

"What are *you* talking about? Until this morning, you and Kyle never would have been seen with me. And sure, maybe I shouldn't have accepted it so easily, but it's not like I have anyone else waiting for me at school. I thought maybe we could be real friends. But all you've done is grill me about Kayla. If you're so obsessed with her, go back to being her friend."

"We were never friends!" I yell. I can't catch my breath. The more I try to convince Kim of this, the less I believe it myself. Memories are cutting into my vision, me with Kayla and Hannah. Laughing like friends do. I jam my fists into my eye sockets, hoping to block them out.

"Are you kidding me? You, Kayla and Hannah were BFFs. The popular girls. You wouldn't be caught dead with me at a party. See?" Kim shifts in her chair, tilting her computer screen towards me.

There's a picture of me, squished in between Kayla and Hannah at a table in the cafeteria. Huge smiles on our faces. Kayla pinching my chin, planting a big kiss on my cheek. We look like best friends. Like we always have been.

"That's hilarious. Great photoshop skills, Kim," I say, but her eyebrows draw together and there's another pang in my gut. Another lie falling from my lips that I don't believe.

"You think I'd waste my time giving you a life every other girl here wants? This isn't photoshop. This was taken a few weeks ago, before the party. You three. Best friends." Her voice softens a tad, and she turns to look at me directly. "Look, I don't know what happened between you and Kayla. But you need to talk to her about it. Not me. Not anyone else. You two are the only ones who can sort this out."

The room is spinning. The faces distorting, long blurry unrecognizable people surrounding me with big eyes and gaping mouths. I clench my fists, digging my nails into my palms with enough force to ground me. To bring me back.

I take a few steadying breaths, though I feel anything but

steady.

"Thank you, Kim. For your help. I'm… I'm sorry. If what you say is true, I was never overly nice to you, and I'm sorry."

She gives me a sad smile and a little shrug, like my words don't matter, they just fall right off her and make no difference.

I quickly head for the door. I cast another look at Ms. Walker and her lips are a thin red line that I can't read. I expect her to reprimand me now, for causing a scene and not being where I should be. But she just narrows her eyes and then shifts them back down to the book that she's reading. I catch a glimpse of the title—*Never Let Me Go* by Kazuo Ishiguro—and though I've never read it, or seen it before for that matter, it seems strikingly familiar.

My head is a web of thoughts and memories stuck together. I need to pry them apart. Figure out what is happening to me.

The squeak of my leather shoes echo through the empty hallway. I embrace the false sense of safety and head to my locker. Even if nothing happened between me and Kayla's boyfriend, it's clear that she—and the entire school—think something did. And I'm not sure what kind of wrath Kayla will bring forth, but I do know that I don't want to be around to find out.

I throw my books into my locker, the door blocking out the natural light filling the hallway. I want to fade into the shadow, tuck myself away for a minute until I can make sense of what is going on.

I brace myself for my next class, hoping to take shelter in the safety of a crowded classroom. But when I slam my locker shut, the hallway isn't as bright as it should be. A shadow is cast, stretching down from one end of the hall to where I'm standing.

In the shape of a girl.

My heart races and I swear Kayla can smell my fear because the corner of her mouth twitches up into a threatening smirk.

"Alexandra, I think we need to have a little chat," she calls down the hallway. I most definitely do not want to chat, at least not until I can figure out what is going on.

"No thanks! Gotta run!" I yell, turning on my heel and racing towards the other end of the hallway where there's a large door to freedom waiting for me.

I glance back to make sure Kayla isn't coming after me, and she's not. She's standing rigid at the other end of the hall with someone else.

My mom.

# TWENTY-SIX

**I BURST OUT OF** the school into a cloud of skunky smoke, which sends me into a hysterical coughing fit. I keel over, my hands on my knees, eyes watering with every cough.

"Woaaahhhh, easy man," a voice with large hands clumsily thumps me on my back. It's supposed to be helping but it decidedly does not.

I jolt upright into the squinted eyes of Brian. He's pulled back into his oversize blazer, his button up disheveled and untucked. His hair has grown out of the Academy's standard and he's trying to hide it with a bright orange beanie. Not exactly the most subtle.

"You good?" He asks as tears run down my face. I've finally caught my breath but was not expecting to be derailed. I whip around to the door to make sure I wasn't followed, but the coast is clear. "You running from someone?"

"Kayla," I push out and my voice cracks. "Apparently she

wants to like, kick my ass."

"But you guys are like, besties," Brian mocks, leaning back against the brick wall, though he's not looking at me. He's not looking anywhere in particular.

"Rude. Also rude, she seems to think I was making out with her man at your party," I confide, maybe a little more accusatory than necessary. Just because it was Brian's party, doesn't mean it's his fault.

He lets out a childish giggle. "No way, man. The only spit that dude was tasting was Kayla's." Another giggle and some rustling as Brian reaches into his blazer pocket for a pen-shaped object. "You weren't even there long enough to talk to him. You caught one glimpse of his buddy and bolted."

"Wait, what? For real?" If that's true, then Kayla needs to STFU and apologize.

"Yeah man," he nods, again not looking at me. "I see everything."

Brian's questionable coherency aside, this is the best information I've got out of anyone.

"Thanks, Bri!" I call over my shoulder, already jogging around the school to the side entrance.

We never use these doors; this is where the stoners hang out—clearly—and where trucks make deliveries to our cafeteria. Even though all the food is cringe, no one has ever cared where it came from. I guess all they had to do was hang out back. It's hard to miss the giant ass truck sitting in the loading dock with a bright red logo stamped on its side.

TrueWood Cola Co.

I swear the name is familiar, but no idea where I would have seen it before. There's a man with a trolley carefully unloading crates marked COLA under the strict supervision of our lunch manager, Carol. I've always liked Carol; she always slips me some extra seasoning or cheese to the slop she knows is almost inedible. I wave to her, pretending I am just going about my normal business. She doesn't return it, just stares at me and my stomach drops.

The side entrance opens to Mom's office. I hope she dragged Kayla back here by her bleach blond hair for a lecture on stalking her daughter through the hall. I close the heavy fire door quietly behind me, cushioning it so it doesn't slam.

The little lobby area outside of Mom's office is by far the quietest place in school. Which is why the giant lost and found bin is bursting with smelly gym shoes, abandoned clothes and lost bags. Nothing is worth saving if it means risking a run in with my mom, apparently.

I make my way around the bin, closer to her office. Muffled voices crawl through the gap between floor and door and I swear I hear my name in Mom's mouth. Something sour she spits out.

A knife of anxiety strikes through my chest. Her tone slashing.

My chest tightens and I brace, need to run. But it's my mom, not some Stranger Danger. What is going on with me?

An ear-piercing scrape echoes in the din of the lobby, chairs against linoleum floor, as the bodies inside shuffle to a stand. My ear is nearly pressed up to the wooden door and I jolt back in surprise.

She can't find me Nancy Drew-ing around the school when I should be in class. I look desperately for somewhere to hide. The janitor's closet stinks of stale water and oil-drenched rags, but it's the only quick option. I push myself in next to a dirty mop bucket and overcrowded shelves, closing the door tightly behind me just as the other door opens.

Harsh heels slap against the floor, then her unmistakable voice.

"Ok, back to class, keep your mouth shut. Got it?" Her words are scolding, even though she's not talking to me.

Her shrill voice a siren song, goosebumps rise to the surface of my arms. I stumble further back in the closet, nails scratching against the floor to push me further and further in. It's a small space, but not suffocating.

The small space isn't suffocating, it's comforting. A safe haven. Something tugs at me…

My mom is right outside the door. I suck in my breath, don't bat an eye, wait for the closet door to be yanked open, but nothing happens.

"What a mess," she mumbles, likely picking through the lost and found bin. I make myself smaller as she rustles through the items.

High pitched tones pierce the quiet and I jump. A phone. It's just a phone. I level my breath, shifting slightly so I am able to hear.

"Yes, I would say we do have a problem." That tone again. The response is muffled, but deep. A man, likely. "You can't possibly think that's true."

That edge cuts into me again. A wound cracks open, flashes of memories seeping out.

*Memories of her voice breaking through my closet door, my small kid hands clasped over my ears, my eyes closed very, very tightly. And the fear that built in my chest. I used to spend a lot of time hiding in closets as a kid. Shelter from the outside world. From my mother and her harsh, hurtful words. Cramming myself into a quiet ball, the thoughts seep back into my mind.*

Adrenaline pumps. Mouth clamps shut. A little girl, terrified of her own mother. That same girl, so many years later, just as afraid.

"No, I don't know where she went! She used to do this all the time as a child, brat that she was. No, I don't think she knows much yet. We have to contain this situation before it gets out of control again… yes, fine, I'll be there in 20."

She ends the call and stomps over to her office door, but I don't hear it open. She must be standing there, listening, and I pray to anything and everything that she won't come back over to the closet. When I don't think I can hold my breath any longer, her office door opens and then slams shut behind her.

Only then do I dare to breathe.

# TWENTY-SEVEN

**KAYLA AND I ARE** only in one class together, and it just so happens that is where I'm supposed to be right now. I tear down the hall towards Calculus. I'm clearly annoying everyone as I run by, knocking into them without apology. I feel completely out of control, and I wonder whether this is what it's like.

If this is the first stage of going wild.

I burst into the classroom and all the heads turn to me at once. Kayla's in her usual seat. Perfectly poised, not a worry in the world.

I rush in, straight up to her desk, but she scoffs and makes a big show of looking away. Annoyance. Lingering anger. I open my mouth to explain—explain what, who the eff knows—but the bell has rung, and Mr. Cross is glaring at me pointedly, waiting for me to sit down.

Kayla doesn't look at me once the entire class. I want to cry.

I want to scream. What the hell is going on with her, with this school, with me? The whole hour is torture, questions burning my tongue, anxiety nipping at the ends of my fingers. As soon as the bell rings, Kayla is up and out of the room. I grab my shit and run after her.

"Kayla, wait up!" I yell, but she doesn't stop. Students move out of her way like some choreographed flash mob, quickly rushing back in on me when I try to follow in her wake. I push, make my elbows sharp. I can almost hear more rumors spring to life in their heads. Juicy details to add to the rhetoric already spreading about me.

I corner Kayla at her locker. Her back is to me as she aggressively throws books into it. The slamming makes my head throb. My vision blurs.

I grab her arm to get her attention and she whirls on me, her eyes raging.

"Leave me alone!" She spits and the words hit hard.

*Broken windshield against my face. A deer.*
*No, not a deer.*

"Kayla, we need to talk." It's all I can get out before she yanks her arm. "Kayla!" Students pretend not to stare, cameras at their hip. Subtle.

Paparazzi, hoping for things to escalate.

This morning, I was her prey. Now she won't even look at me. The only thing that could have changed is my mother.

Whatever she said in her office.

My heart warms. Lioness protecting her cub.

Hannah takes a corner too fast, slipping across the well-worn hall. Her hair is more frizz than curl. She's lacking the usual cardigan and her stack of bracelets are bouncing uncontrollably as she hurries down the hall. They're hypnotizing, the way they catch the light. I'm staring, so it's hard to miss the angry marks that they hide.

"Kayla, what's going on?" She puts herself directly between us, head bobbing back and forth.

"Ask this betch. Chasing me down like a rabid fangirl. Bloody hell." Kayla sneers, glaring at me with such a cutting look that I take a step back.

"OMG. Look, I know what you think happened, like what everyone's saying, but I swear I can explain. Well, I think I can. Okay, I can't explain exactly, but seriously, I did not make out with your boyfriend!" Hands shaking. Tongue thick. I don't know how to convince her.

People crowd around us. Some idiot yells "cat fight," and a few others answer with hisses and meows. I don't have time for these nimrods, and apparently Hannah doesn't either.

"Alright, lots of tension here," Hannah raises her hands in a calming motion, like we're wild animals ready to attack. "Let's… take this somewhere a little more private, shall we? Sort this all out?"

As if on cue, the doors behind us open and Ms. Walker steps out of the library. She looks at us expectantly, like she was waiting for us. Was she waiting for us?

"Girls, come on in," Ms. Walker says sternly, not giving us a choice. Kayla and I obediently listen, following Hannah through the open doors.

Hannah takes a seat at the round table in the middle of the library. She pats her hands on the table, gesturing for us to join her. I wait for Kayla to move first. If she'll leave or acknowledge me or keep freezing me out. But there's no dramatics, she just sits down, face blank.

"It's about time we all had a talk," Hannah says as Ms. Walker closes the library door. The click of the lock sliding into place is an ominous warning. Nothing good is going to come from this talk.

"Is this an intervention or something?" I ask, half-joking, half-fearful, half expecting my mother to shoot up out of the ground like a specter.

I wait for Ms. Walker to explain, but it's Hannah who finally speaks.

"Listen, this is getting out of control. Everything is a mess. I tried to ease you into things, I tried to drop hints, but we're running out of time, and we can't afford the slow transition anymore." I hear Hannah's words, but they're nothing but noise. I can't make any shape or form of them. Kayla doesn't seem to know what she's talking about either. She's doing the thing where she masks her confusion with annoyance. I'd know it anywhere. Which means I must know her better than I thought I did and maybe Kim wasn't full of shit.

A full minute must go by. Hannah's more than happy to wait out the turning wheels in my brain, but I don't have the patience. "What are you talking about?"

"This, all of this. You and Kayla fighting. You are friends. We are friends," Hannah gestures to us all, spread out around the table. The furthest thing from friends.

"We are *not* friends," Kayla whines.

My eyes roll. I can't help it. "Stubborn cow."

My hands clasp my mouth, as if they can push the words back in. I brace for a punch, a barb, some lashing from Kayla. But relief washes over me the same time her obnoxious laugh does.

"Preppy priss," she says through a smile.

Actors in a play, following lines, falling back into our roles. A familiarity building back between us. I can't ignore it. Everything about her that drives me up the wall, coated with the feeling of a protector. A savior. A friend.

"Okay…" I heave a sigh. Kayla doesn't look away from me now and my heart settles back in my chest. "Let's say that is true, that Kayla and I are friends. Why don't I remember that? Why do I think Kim and Kyle have been my best friends since I started here? That doesn't make sense," I ask. It should be a simple question, not the thread that is going to unravel my entire life.

Hannah takes a deep, steadying breath.

"Kayla, how did you first hear that Alexandra made out with Andy?" Hannah looks to Kayla, who seems to be more interested in everything else in the room but this conversation.

"Someone posted in the Pine Cliff WhatsApp group. It was

anonymous, but then everyone else added to it, saying that they saw you and Andy together, confirming the details," Kayla admits.

"This all started from an anonymous message in a group text? And you believed it, over me? Seriously?" I roll my eyes again, disbelief.

"What, I thought it was some kind of *Gossip Girl* thing." Kayla looks sheepish, embarrassed, at least.

Now it's my turn to take a steadying breath. I press my palms into the top of the table, trying to calm myself. My entire life is on trial because of an anonymous message.

"Can we all agree that Alexandra did not make out with Andy?" Hannah plays middleman again, slowly smoothing out the waves of our little friend group.

"Fine, alright? I believe you," Kayla finally says, staring intently at her fingernails like they're the most interesting things in the world. "But if you didn't, why would someone say that? They knew it was going to start shit." She asks the million-dollar question.

We both look at Hannah, waiting for her to brilliantly provide the answers, but she says nothing. Just stares at me.

"I don't know who sent it!" I say, exasperated, but I realize that may not be entirely true. This whole situation, a mysterious message pitting my best friend against me, it's eerily familiar. A dangling memory, my first year of high school, back before the accident. Something almost exactly the same with a new group of friends. "Wait, I think… this might have happened before?"

"And if this happened before, who was behind it then?" Hannah asks, more pointedly this time and immediately, I picture her in my head. My mother. But no, that can't be right. Why would she do that?

"That's not possible. My mother wouldn't…" I say it out loud this time, giving Hannah the chance to contradict me. To tell me I'm being ridiculous. When she doesn't, my heart sinks deeper into my chest. A reality I've forgotten comes crawling back up to the surface. "But why… how could…."

I snap my eyes shut, try to push the thoughts from my mind but they take hold, shake me, scream at me to wake up.

"Hannah, what is going on, you're freaking me out." But she isn't the one freaking me out, it's these memories, slipping back to the forefront of my mind. My mother, years of an unhappy childhood, never being enough, carrying all her blame for killing my father.

"My father…" it slips out of my mouth the moment it comes into frame in my mind. Hannah sits up a little straighter in her chair. I'm looking around the room wildly, like I expect him to show up. But Ms. Walker is the only adult in the room, standing just off to the side while my entire life implodes. "The accident, the deer…" The words are wrong. Something tugs at my thoughts. "I was driving, there was a deer…" I try again, but again, it doesn't seem right. "Was there a deer? Didn't I kill my father?" It's rhetorical, but Hannah's face, even Ms. Walker's, tells me that this is the question I should have been asking since we sat down.

The right words find me, pushed out in panicked breaths. "I

didn't kill my father, I wasn't driving. The accident, my mother was driving, and she lost control of the car. I didn't kill him."

The words pour out of me along with all the grief and blame and self-hatred that had burrowed into the curves of my shoulders. It all makes sense now, the things that weren't making sense. My mother's subtle jabs, the resentment in her eyes. It wasn't because my father is dead, it's because I'm alive and he isn't.

"How could I not remember that? How could I not remember how my mother made me feel? How is this possible?" I was young, but there are memories that come back to me now. Long, empty weeks where I ate nothing but cereal and crackers because there was no food on the table. The scent of rotting garbage and strong body odor. My mother strewn on the couch, her limp hand hanging off the side barely clutching a near-empty glass of honeyed liquid. Stumbling around in a daze, never looking straight at me. Or worse, looking at me with pure hatred.

*It hurts to be awake. There's nothing worth being awake for.*

Until he came back. This happening, over and over again, until it didn't. Until a family trip gone wrong. When he died, and we moved. She said I was nothing. That it was all my fault.

I suck in a breath. Tears press against the back of my eyes, hands starting to tremor. "Whatever is happening here, she has something to do with it, doesn't she?"

Hannah bites her lip, looking over at Ms. Walker. Kayla doesn't miss their exchange, but she leaves me the floor. What do you say after that, anyway? I let out a laugh. It's more of a maniacal snort that draws everyone's attention. "I'm sorry. I just… my mother is steamrolling my entire existence. And I had no idea. I've never questioned her. I'm so embarrassed. So ashamed…" I trail off.

"Don't be ashamed. Be angry!" Ms. Walker steps up to the table and reaches for my hand, but I pull it away quickly. It's shaking, and I don't want her to know how much this has affected me. "You were a child. You're still a child. And your mother was manipulating you, gaslighting you. And she still is. But it's not your fault. None of this is your fault."

"Ugh! What is Ms. Walker even doing here?" Kayla's words are an explosion in the quiet of the library, stealing back the attention.

"You don't think I could do all this on my own, do you? Keep track of everyone, know what is really going on with the Academy…" Hannah's words are soft, a gentle look of admiration to Ms. Walker, who has spent too many years with Kayla to seem fazed by her attitude.

"What do you mean keep track of everyone? What *is* going on with the Academy?" Kayla keeps shooting accusatory looks at Ms. Walker and I take the opportunity to study her. She's only been my teacher for a few months, but she seems to always be around when something goes down. Carrying herself with a wise confidence, dark eyes that know more than they let on. She can't be much older than us, a couple of years, if that. But familiar. A tiredness weighing on her that we're all fighting right about now.

"Not everything is as it seems around here, Kayla. You should know that by now," Hannah says. Ms. Walker puts a hand on Hannah's shoulder, looking back and forth between Kayla and me.

"Like me, for example," Ms. Walker continues. "The school knows me as Bree Walker, but my real name is Bree Tran. Though you're probably better acquainted with my sister—Emily."

# TWENTY-EIGHT

**THE NAME CARVES ITSELF** out in my mind. Bree Tran. The small resemblance to an old ghost story tugging at the edges. Emily Tran, going wild and jumping off the cliff behind the Academy.

A girl flashes in my mind. Long plaited hair, a haunted look. I don't know how, but I know without a doubt that it's Emily Tran. Bree is older, a little more weathered. Hair a sleek bob, but she has the same lost and lonely glossed-over eyes as Emily's. It's easy to see the closeness between the two if you know what to look for. But with a different name, a different style, Bree could slip right under the Academy's nose and position herself right at the center of whatever is going on here.

Bree watches me, a small smirk at the corner of her dark lips. "You look like you've seen a ghost."

"Emily was your sister?" I ask, dumbfounded.

"Emily *is* my sister," is what she responds with, and I take a second to realize what she's telling me.

"Emily is supposed to be dead." I say, echoing the ghost story everyone at the school has heard.

"So are you." Bree closes the space between us, coming to stand right in front of me. "You can't believe everything you hear, Alexandra. It makes a great urban legend, something to tell around the fire, but none of it's true."

"So, she didn't go wild and jump off the cliff behind the school?" I ask. Kayla's mouth is hanging as wide open as mine probably is.

"Oh no, she went wild. That's where all of this starts. My sister figured it all out. She tried to tell everyone what was really going on, and they threw her in one of those cells in the basement. But there were already whispers, people who had started questioning what was happening at this school. What is still happening. There are people, lurking in the shadows, trying to help where they can. They helped me free my sister. She's safe, away from this place."

"But you're still here …" I say, wondering how many others are involved. Of all the people rumored to go wild at this school. If all those people who disappeared managed to escape…

"I couldn't just walk away, let this keep happening to people like Emily. To people like you. Like with everyone, their before life is erased. There's no record of a sister in Emily's file, no trace of me here. So, I stayed. And I've been trying to help guide you students as best I can."

Hannah looks at me with sad, soft eyes before reaching into her bag and pulling out a stack of white papers. She slowly slides it across the table towards me. Words are scribbled across the front in tilted handwriting that is undoubtedly my own.

## THE REAL ALEXANDRA SHAW

"What is this..." I start, but Hannah nudges the pages towards me again and I open them, afraid and anxious about what I'll read.

Letters and lines float around on the page in front of me until my mind snaps them into order. A medical file. I flip through the pages, reading through the words as everybody stares at me. "I don't understand what any of this means. Memory distortion and replacement? There is an entire page about overlapping memories with fabrications" I look around the table. Hannah doesn't seem phased, but Kayla's eyes are wide, matching my own. Hannah reaches into her bag again and pulls out more folded papers and slides them towards Kayla.

"No way. Get that garbage away from me," she says, pushing them back towards Hannah. Hannah pleads with her, explaining to her why it's important for her to see the words for herself. I try to tune them out, flipping through the rest of my own pages.

The last one is a discharge statement. My first name printed clearly at the top, but this Alexandra has a different last name. Holland. Her birthday is the same as mine, but the year is wrong. It says they discharged her to the Academy, under the care of her mother, to be monitored by Headmaster Johnson, almost a full year ago.

Which can't be right because that's my story. But the timeline doesn't add up, these dates aren't what are in my head. This girl has been out of the hospital for almost a year, not a few months. This girl is eighteen, not seventeen.

If this is supposed to be me, I'm missing almost a year of my life.

My head hurts. I'm trying desperately to put the pieces together, to remember my time in the hospital after the accident. Everything's just out of reach, if I can only push a little harder, reach a little further.

"Ugh, why can't I remember!" It breaks through my lips, and I want to rip out my hair in frustration.

"It's what they do, they make it so you don't remember the bad things. So, you can start a new life and be happier." Hannah's words still me. There's truth in them, but it's taking a while for everything to come clearly to the surface. "The Institute. They take in people who have been hurt, who have almost died. They save them and then overwrite their memories with new ones. Rewire their learned reactions, even their goals and priorities. Try to erase the path that led them to their end, to save them from a similar fate again."

No wonder I have no idea who I am, what I like, what I want to do with my life. All the pieces that are supposed to come together to build a person. Everything that at one point made me, *me* has been turned into what someone else wants me to be.

"What do you mean it's what they do? It's what who do? What bad things? I don't have any bad things in my life, unless you count that summer I spent with Ryan whatshisname. That was a total mistake." Kayla is rambling, her breath short and quick. She might be on the verge of a panic attack.

"Kayla, breathe," Hannah encourages. "Try to think. What do you remember after Brian's party?"

She answers almost immediately. "I woke up Saturday, a little hungover, got that message in WhatsApp and spent the rest of the weekend planning my revenge on Alexandra." She says it so casually I can't help but laugh.

Kayla shrugs, smiling as well, but it's wiped away the minute Hannah rests her hand on Kayla's arm. I know Kayla feels it too, the calm before the storm. That small second of stillness before everything explodes. "That party wasn't Friday night, Kay. It was over a week ago. You haven't been at school for a week. Neither of you."

Kayla goes unnaturally quiet. "Please tell me what is going on. What happened to us?"

My brain has finally caught up, strange words starting to flow out of my mouth, explanations that I didn't realize I had. "A medical Institute. I think I was there before I moved here. And again, the other night, after I figured out what they did to me the first time..." I trail off, the words setting in, taking hold of me. "There's a boy… from the party. I wasn't with Andy; I was with him. I knew him before…"

When I trail off, Kayla pushes me. "What boy? We know all

the boys here. You always say that they're too boring and all the same."

Kayla's eyebrows curl in and she looks at me as she realizes what she said. Something about me, about us, coming naturally from her mind proving that we were, as Hannah said, friends.

"He doesn't go here. I don't know who he is. I don't even know his name..."

"His name is Logan." Hannah's whisper is soft, but strong, a confidence rare for her. "The boy you met is named Logan."

It's our turn to stare at her.

"We don't know a boy named Logan," Kayla answers for me.

"No, but you did. You both did, though Alexandra has known him for much longer. He calls you Lex."

*Lex, is that you?*

My head shakes, rattling everything around inside. None of this makes sense, but something inside me shifts. Pieces that have been shook loose are dragging themselves back into place, bringing with it an old familiar feeling.

"But why me?" Kayla interrupts, clearly having a hard time with this. "What do I have to do with this? It sounds like this is Alexandra's problem, it's her and this boy they are focused on. What do I have to do with any of this?"

"Because you were at the party with Logan. To erase him, to make sure that no one mentioned him to Alexandra and trigger her old memories again, they had to erase everyone who saw him.

Including you."

"But you were at the party too! Why didn't they erase you?" Kayla is pleading, as if she can somehow reverse time and none of this will be true.

"They did. But they've reset me so many times it doesn't work anymore. That's something I never let them know, of course. I pretend to be whatever they need me to be. It's easy to stay under the radar when you're the quiet, mousy girl. No one suspects anything."

Ms. Walker—Bree—picks up so easily whenever Hannah stops talking. They've obviously been working together for a long time. There's a trust and comfort between them that makes me ache with longing. "Not everyone gets triggered easily, most people are so removed from their old life that they're still on their first procedure from the Institute. But for whatever reason, you keep triggering, Alexandra. Logan keeps popping up in your life, and the overwriting, it starts to slip, doesn't take hold of the original memory as strongly. Double vision, two realities for one person. Usually this is where people go wild, they can't handle the confusion. But for some people, they don't know why, the mind sorts itself out. It learns, it remembers, so each time it happens, it gets easier."

Me: Eighteen, apparently—missing one year of my life. Favorite Color: Not pink, that was implanted in a laboratory. Favorite singer: Not Taylor Swift, which was influenced by something someone gave me. Does any of this even matter? Not when I can't tell what is mine anymore.

I'm splitting into two people, someone who is real and someone who is not.

Once a little piece is pulled from the void, there's no stopping the rest of the repressed memories from coming barreling towards the surface. Their dark hands take hold of me again and I'm reminded of my mother, of all the pain, all the sadness. Logan fully re-enters, my knight in shining armor swooping in and showing me that I am worthy of love. But everything is cast in shadows, and it drags me deeper and deeper back to a place I'm not sure I want to return to. All these wild, unhappy thoughts that significantly change who I am.

Kayla has her eyes crunched closed, working and reworking the moments of her own life. I wonder whether she is struggling with her past in the same way.

"I don't want to remember my life before," she finally says as if reading my mind. "I mean, I'm happy. I love my life here. I love my friends. We're graduating next year. If what you are saying, if all this stems from trauma or pain or, bloody hell, death, then I don't want to know. I don't want this to change. Is that bad?"

Hannah shakes her head. "Everyone has their own way of processing, of knowing what they need. If you don't want to remember, who are we to question that, to make you?"

"I wish you never told me this. Why did you have to tell me this?" Kayla whispers, putting her head in her hands, trying to hold herself together.

"So why now?" I ask. "If you couldn't tell us everything before, if you were worried about triggering our old memories, why are you telling us now?"

"You are all here to test the Institute's procedure in the real world, with real world stimulants and triggers." The seriousness of the situation is heavy in Bree's voice. "The experiment is a failure, Alexandra. People keep triggering, memories keep slipping. It's not good for business and they need to fix that."

"And what does that mean… for us?" I ask, realizing what she's really saying. What are they going to do with the pieces of their failed experiment?

"We don't know, but we don't want to take any risks. That's why we need to move quickly, get as many of you self-aware again as possible."

"And how do we do that? What are we supposed to do now?" I look between Hannah and Bree. Searching for answers, waiting for orders. I'm a part of all of this now, whether I want to be or not.

"Now, we fight back." Bree says, leaning over the table.

If I weren't already sitting, my legs would completely give out. How strange my entire life has become. How I am part of this experiment, this conspiracy. How I am joining this little whisper network of survivors to help free the other students.

I can't do this, I'm no vigilante.

I'm just a girl.

Bree can apparently read my mind, pick up on my hesitance, because she lets out an annoyed sigh. "You need to wake up, girl. Stop trying to convince yourself that this isn't your fight. You of all people should be raging, be the first in line to take that place down. You have spent a good portion of your life thinking you killed someone. That is messed up! You need to be more furious. You need to find something to fight for." Her eyes bore into mine. "So, do you? Have something to fight for?"

The obvious answer is Logan. That's who I'm fighting to get back to. But that's not what fuels me, that's not what will carry me through this. I think of my mother, the reason I am even here in the first place. The person who, my entire life, has manipulated and controlled everything about me.

"No, not fight for. To fight against." Something shifts in me with those simple words. Something I never had the courage to feel before. Because Bree is right about me being furious. I am furious. And I'm fucking tired. "I'm tired of sitting back and letting whatever happens happen to me. I'm ready to start fighting. To start taking back some control."

If I ever want to see the other side of this. If I ever want to be free.

We've been holed up in the library for what seems like hours. A lifetime unraveling in front of me, memories slipping back in.

I don't know where Logan is, if he made it back to school, if he would even remember me. Does my mother know I know what happened to me? The only thing I do know is that I can't forget. I won't forget. Kayla may be happy with her new life, but I won't let my old one disappear. I won't let everything that I am disappear. "I need to find Logan. Whatever is going on, he's involved in this too. I lost him once; I will not lose him again." I search for my phone, pat my jeans, tear through my bag. I've lost it, again. Or more likely, it's been taken. "I don't know how to get a hold of him. As far as my life goes, Logan doesn't exist for me."

"Logan doesn't matter," Bree huffs her words a slap. "Hannah and I have been working hard to flip people inside the school and bring them back to themselves before they go wild or get reset again. Our network is getting bigger, it won't be long before we can stand up to the Academy. To the Institution, even.

To make all this public and shut this program down for good. We have to stick to the plan." Her fists are on her hips, an authoritative stance, but I'm done bowing down to authority.

"That's fine. You do what you have to do. But if you want my help, I'm not doing anything until I know that Logan is safe." I stand, mimicking Bree's confidence. She may not be much older than me, but she's taller than me and would absolutely overpower me in a fight. If it came to that.

I look to Hannah. Sweet, gentle Hannah, who has always come to my rescue when I've needed her most.

"I don't have his number, but Andy would." She says, ignoring the way Bree throws her hands in the air in frustration.

"Yes! Andy. I'll ask him for it." Kayla jumps up from the table, pulling out her phone. She quickly types out a message and we wait, idle, hoping for a quick response. When her phone dings, her eyebrows crease. I move closer and read the text over her shoulder.

**Andy**
Who's Logan?

"What does he mean, who is Logan?" I ask, but she's already typing.

**Kayla**
U r mate Logan.
Alexandra saw him at party
& freaked the F out

**Andy**
Remember party.
No Logan. ???

"Go to Andy's Instagram page, there are photos of Logan there, you can screen cap and send it." Kayla does as I suggest, bringing up Andy's page. She scrolls down to the photos of Andy tossing around the football. Leaning against a tree. Wrestling with his friends. But Logan is gone. I grab her phone and scroll through every photo again. There's no sign of Logan in any of the little squares.

"Are you sure there was a photo?" Kayla asks and for a minute, I'm not sure. Was there a photo? Is that something else I've misremembered?

"What do you think this means?" I ask, happy that Hannah is too busy arguing with Bree and Kayla is too busy scrolling through her phone because I don't want the answer. If Andy doesn't know Logan, if he doesn't seem to exist at Carver, then where could he be? I drop back down into my chair, everything suddenly hitting at once. Because there's only one place he could be.

The Institute has Logan.

# TWENTY-NINE

**"ALEXANDRA, ARE YOU SURE** about this? It seems a little...
rash. Maybe Bree's right and we should stick to the plan?" Hannah
says as we sneak down the hallway towards Mr. Johnson's office.
He's a connection between the Academy and the Institute. He's a
connection between me and Logan. His office might have
something we can use to get to Logan. To rescue him before it's
too late.

"I want nothing more than to help you rescue Logan but
finding him at school was one thing. This is too risky—we don't
know the first thing about breaking into an institute. And what
about the people there, they would be in various states of
overwriting. What if we disturb them, what if we accidentally
cause them to go wild?"

"What else are we supposed to do, Hannah? Just leave him?
Abandon him? Would you do that to me? To Kayla?" At the

mention of her name, Kayla grunts. She's following us on our rescue mission, but we may as well have tied her up and forced her at gun point. "It's my fault he's there. My fault he's part of this at all. I know that it's selfish, that I'm putting him—me—before everyone else. But I need to find him before they reset him. I can't be responsible for someone else getting hurt." My voice cracks and I squeeze those thoughts and fears back down.

"Okay. I get it. I trust you. Whatever you want to do, we're with you. We'll find him, we'll get him back. I promise." Hannah whispers, reaching a hand over to grab mine. Kayla makes no effort to include herself in the moment, in my reassurance, she just stalks off ahead of us down the empty hall.

"Mr. Johnson should be meeting with Bree..." Hannah pushes up the bracelets on her arm to see her watch more clearly. All I see are the scars there. How did I miss them before? "... right about now to discuss your behavior. Which means all we have to do is get into his office, have a quick look around and see if there is anything we can use to get into the Institute."

So calm. So collected. The Hannah I know would curl in on herself, shying away from taking the lead. But this Hannah is stepping up, taking control. With fire in her eyes, she holds herself taller, more confidently than I have ever seen before. Pure determination.

I shake my head at the deceit of it all. "You had me fooled, you know. I never would have expected, never would have known you were part of this whole underground movement" I whisper, nudging Hannah with my elbow. She gives me a proud little smirk.

"You aren't the only one she fooled," Kayla grumbles ahead of us, where she's still sulking. She's hasn't been able to look Hannah in the eye since we found everything out.

"Kayla, I wanted to tell you… I tried to tell you! Giving you subtle hints, but you never wanted to look at any of the books I gave you…" Hannah trails off when Kayla doesn't respond.

Hannah gives me a helpless look, begging forgiveness and understanding, but all I can do is shrug and continue down the hallway. Classes are still in session; the school is a ghost town. Eerie, after the chaos of this morning. People everywhere, waiting for me to get my ass kicked by Kayla.

"How did they find you, or recruit you, or whatever? They can't like, pull you aside in the hallway and say that you've been brainwashed." I ask, like that is the most ridiculous thing of this whole situation.

"It starts small. Posters left around the school or other places the Institute uses." On cue, Hannah points to the bulletin board on the wall beside us. Bright posters advertise an upcoming school dance, counselling sessions, clubs. "We call them 'trigger words.' Phrases that make you think. Like 'Wake up' or 'Remember.' If someone sees a message enough, it implants in the brain, you can't shake it. If someone focuses on these phrases, the hope is that they will start to question some of the things around them. If you know what to look for, the Academy is covered in messages." As Hannah says it, I flash back to Brian's party, Scott's basement, the flier in my locker. Neon colors have painted the hallways of our school for as long as I can remember, I just never paid enough attention. Never knew what I was right in front of me this whole time.

"Sure, what they're doing it is wrong. But can you tell me there isn't even a little bit of you that thinks that maybe we are better off forgetting those bad parts? Forgetting all the pain, all the bad memories?" Kayla says, startling us both. Her first words in ages.

Hannah turns to look at Kayla, trying to connect, but she's still avoiding her as if none of this is real. "You can take away the pain, but it's that pain that gives you fire, gives you drive. The pain doesn't define you, it's how you react to it that does. You take away the pain and there's nothing left."

When we reach Headmaster Johnson's office, the door is closed, which hopefully means he's gone to meet with Bree as planned.

"Do you have a key?" I ask Hannah, who shakes her head, holding out her student ID card. "You had the keys to the locked cells beneath the school, but expect me to break into the headmaster's office with that? Come on, this isn't a movie."

She swats me with the ID card. "Just shove it in the crack of the door until it presses the little latch thing. Easy."

There is no way this is going to work.

With a steady hand, I shove the corner of the card between the door and the frame. It takes some wiggling, but I get it in there. I push the other corner of the card into the slot so that the whole edge of the card is between the door and the frame.

"Okay, now what?" I ask, staring at the card, Hannah's

picture cut in half by the door frame.

"Bend and slide it further into the door so that it presses down the lever." Hannah says as if it's the easiest thing in the world. It's not. I bend and push and wiggle and nothing happens.

"Ugh, here, you are useless," Kayla impatiently shoves me aside. She grabs the card and pushes it so hard until there's a loud *snap*.

"Please tell me that was the door unlatching and not you breaking my student ID in half?" Hannah sighs as Kayla turns around holding half the ID card out to her.

"Sorry?" Kayla shrugs, handing over the broken card. At least she isn't sulking anymore. I reach into my bag for my own ID and try again.

When I get the card inserted into the door, I try bending and pushing with a bit more finesse. There's a soft CLICK and then the door swings open.

"Success!" I exclaim, a little too loudly, but the hall is still empty as we pile into Headmaster Johnson's office.

It's a wonder Headmaster Johnson is such a hardass, his office is lit. Bookshelves line the walls, placed perfectly above rows of filing cabinets. All the books are neatly arranged with display items and pull-out storage boxes in between. His desk has a giant live-edge surface with industrial legs framing built in cubbies and a giant leather desk chair on wheels. There are two white puffy seats on the opposite side of the desk for guests.

It's a beautiful disaster, given there are far too many nooks and crannies for us to rifle through. I dig through his desk first while Kayla and Hannah start inspecting the bookshelf. Opening drawers, leafing through papers. I figure if I find something that has to do with the Academy or the Institute, it can't hurt to have more evidence. But there's nothing that seems important. His laptop is open on his desk, the screen dark. I jiggle the mouse to wake it, but it only offers me a sign in screen and I'm not about to try to crack his password.

I scan the room again, hoping for something to jump out at me, when I see the coat rack in the corner behind the door. There's a white lab coat hanging on a hook, the only item of clothing. I have never seen him wear it at school, so I check the pockets. At first, it's only lint and change. But in the inside breast pocket, I can already tell before reaching in, is what we need.

I pull it out and Headmaster Johnson's serious face leers at me. It's the same face he wears at school when lecturing us on obedience and listening to our elders. The ID badge has a logo at the top, a building with text in a half circle around it—TrueWood Medical Institute. This is what we need to get into the Institute. This is what will help me find Logan.

"I got it! Let's go!" I whisper-yell to the others as I palm the badge. I turn to hurry from the office and nearly slam right into Scott as he lumbers in the doorway.

"What are you doing?" His words pin me in place, even though he looks past me, lingering on Hannah. She shifts behind me, but I can't tell if she's cowering or standing up in defiance.

"Uh—where's the bathroom?" I try to buy some time to think of a believable excuse, but Scott's not dumb.

"You were searching for the bathroom in the school you've gone to for months and accidentally ended up in my father's office?" he says, sarcasm dripping from his words.

"I don't have time to explain, but it's important. I promise!" I say, hoping it'll be enough to win him over. It's not.

"You don't have to explain, I know exactly what you're doing, *Lex*." Scott stands boldly in the doorway, as if he's a security guard of some sort.

"Wait, you called me Lex. Do you know who I am? I mean, who I really am?"

"You mean the girl who burst into my house with her boyband boyfriend, bringing down the terror of the Institute and my father on me? That girl?" He glares at me, but then eases off and lets out a sigh.

"I… don't remember that. But I'm sorry. I really am," I offer genuinely. Hannah and Kayla have joined me in the doorway, and I toy with the thought of whether the three of us could charge him and break through. As if in warning, Scott shifts from one foot to the other, bracing against the door frame making our escape practically impossible.

"You know what he did with my stuff, right? I can't even get into my own basement anymore, thanks to you."

I feel terrible. I know first-hand what it's like to have your identity stripped from you. To be left without the things that you most resonate with.

"I promise, I will make it up to you, but I can't right now. We have to… do something." I move forward again, hoping my momentum will make him move.

"I want in." he says, not moving.

"You don't even know what we're doing," Kayla says, completely confused. She does know what we're doing and wants nothing to do with it.

"I don't know what you're doing, but I know why." He eyes me, waiting, but huffs his impatience instead. "Where do you think Hannah got those medical files, huh?"

Hannah has always had a knack for information finding her.

"If I tell you what we're up to, will you let me keep the badge?" I hold out my hand, the plastic pressed into my palm. He nods. "Alright, but we have to go now. If you're in, you're in. We'll explain on the way."

# THIRTY

**IT TOOK SOME CONVINCING,** but eventually Bree handed over the keys to her car and after a long drive, it's dark when we arrive at the Institute. Not that it matters, we could see the place from miles away, thanks to the bright floodlights. But that means they can see us coming from a mile away, too. I wonder how we're ever going to get in without being seen, but Hannah doesn't take us into the main parking lot.

We drive much further down the road; the Institute getting smaller and smaller behind us. I'm about to ask if we've missed our turn when she finally slows and pulls onto a service road that is nearly grown over with foliage. Anyone driving past would never know it was there. It's another few minutes before we pull off to the side and Hannah shuts off the engine.

"Have you… been here before?" Scott asks. Hannah seems to know her way around this place like it's her summer home.

"By choice or involuntarily? Those are two very different scenarios," she responds, a little smile on her lips, though the reality of the question is nothing to smile at. "I'm sorry, I know this is all still new for you. I've had time to adjust to what is happening here. No, I haven't broken into the Institute before, but Bree is no stranger to how it works here. We've been going over rescue plans for months, just in case."

"Shouldn't Bree be here, then? If she's the expert?" Kayla pipes up from the back seat. Hannah bristles.

"I'm fully capable of leading my own rescue mission, thank you." Her response is curt and Kayla scoffs, rolling her eyes. The air is still thick between them, Kayla not letting go of the grudge and hurt she feels at the reality of our friend's hidden identity.

Hannah shrugs, defeated, and opens the driver's door into the night. We all follow suit, though some of us more begrudgingly than others.

"So, we go in, find where they are keeping Logan, and then we're out. Nothing to it!" I try to lighten the air, but Kayla doesn't look impressed or reassured. Scott isn't very convinced, either, but at least he has the decency to try to hide his doubt as he takes up stride beside Hannah.

We approach the Institute from the rear. It's not as brightly lit back here. I nearly miss the giant fence cutting us off from the door that seems to be our target.

"Hannah, how—" but she shushes me, waving me forward with her hand. I bite my lip and follow closely. She approaches the fence and counts the poles, starting at a trespassing sign. She stops when she reaches four and bends down in front of the pole. There's a scraping noise, a little louder than is probably preferred. Then suddenly, the bottom of the fence peels back wide enough for a body to slip through.

The dirt is cold as I shimmy along it, under the fence. It doesn't take long for us all to make it through and across the grass towards the door. The lock pad is an angry red, and I hold my breath as I bring the stolen pass up to it. After a moment's hesitation, the lock pad turns green, and the door clicks open. Hannah shoots me an accomplished smile. But we aren't done yet, not even close.

"If they can tell that these doors are being opened, we have to make sure we're ready," I tell the back of Hannah's head. She nods, and I prepare myself to run, to hide, to do whatever it takes to track down Logan and get out of here.

We step into a hallway that goes on forever in both directions. Stark white walls dimpled with lock pads, fire extinguishers and mounted first aid kits, as if the people who work here have to be prepared for anything. Everything.

There's minimal signage and large doors on each side with round windows giving a glimpse behind them. My stomach clenches, and I'm not sure I can handle what must be behind each door.

"All we have to do is find what door Logan is behind and get him out. Easy," Hannah tells us, leading the way further down the hallway. Scott follows immediately, sticking close to her. He seems determined to protect her, though that's clearly the last thing she needs. Kayla doesn't move. She's been awfully quiet this whole time. Lips trembling, staring straight ahead, not blinking. I grab her hand, and she jumps.

"Let's do this and get out of here," I whisper to her, but her eyes narrow.

"I can't believe you guys got me into this. I was perfectly fine living in my own simple existence, waiting until graduation when I can go off to college. I don't need to be someone's hero, Alexandra."

"But it's my fault he's here. I need to get him out. We need to know what they're doing here. Maybe we can help others from ending up here too."

"I don't know these people, I don't care about these people, I only care about us getting out of here without getting caught." I'm taken back by Kayla's tone. She's never been the most sympathetic person, but I always thought she was my friend. And isn't this what friends do for each other?

"No one made you come, Kayla," I whisper, though without confidence. If she hears me, she doesn't respond. She roughly knocks her shoulder into me as she pushes past me down the hall after Hannah and Scott.

There are mobile stations scattered throughout the space, one every three or four doors. I try to keep my eyes focused on these stations. Don't think about what I'm passing. Don't think about what I'd see if I was brave enough to peek through one of those windows in the doors.

Hannah is already rummaging through the first station. Scott is mindlessly fumbling with another, but his curiosity is eating at him, and he can't stop looking to the windows. Kayla begrudgingly joins them, but she doesn't even pretend to look for something that will help us find Logan.

I duck into the administrative area, looking for keys or files. Photos hang on the wall, the first of a woman with a stern, tight face. Arms crossed over her chest. I know that look. I know that woman. She cornered us in Scott's basement. A plaque below the photo says Dr. Alice Anderson, Director. Other photos dangle beside her. One of Headmaster Johnson, a plaque below his scowling face claiming Post-Procedure Supervisor.

The last photo on the wall surprises me. Though at this point, it shouldn't. My mother. The plaque below it says Recruitment Liaison Director. No wonder my mother had such input in what's happened to me. Dr. Anderson said so herself, my mother knew everything. I always wondered how she could afford an abrupt move and the tuition for the fancy Academy. But everything was an exchange for being the convincing face people trust when they were approached by the Institute.

Because what parent would be involved in an institute that harmed their own child?

I swallow my anger and start back towards the others. They look at me hopelessly, coming up with even less information than I found.

"Well, let's go door to door?" I whisper-shout, looking up and down the empty hallway. How many hallways of how many rooms on how many floors? This is going to take forever. But the others follow me, Hannah and Scott heading off down different corridors to look into different windows.

I finally bring myself to look into one. Then the next. Searching for Logan and trying to ignore what I find instead. The rooms are the same as in the photograph of me strapped to a metal operating table. Atop these tables are similar human forms, though in varying shapes, sizes, and skin tones. A little plastic rectangle sticks out of each of their heads, a wire running directly from it and into the racks of computers behind them. Kayla huffs behind me, but she follows me down the hall as I keep moving.

"Logan!" I hiss, trying to be loud enough that he will hear me from somewhere beyond these doors.

"Shut up. They're going to hear you." Kayla is about to throttle me. Her eyes scan the surrounding hallway, a heat sensor for movement, anticipating our capture.

"Logan, where are you?" I call again, barging from door to door with Kayla dragging aimlessly behind me. We're halfway down the hall when someone steps out of a corridor I didn't notice, cutting us off from Hannah and Scott.

"Stop where you are!" The voice shatters the stillness. Kayla immediately puts her hands up even though there is no gun. The security guard is young. Sweat builds on his lip, he is so green he has no idea what to do. He looks back and forth between Kayla and me, and Hannah and Scott. His radio hisses, then "Sir, intruders in section D. I repeat, intruders in—"

A hollow clunk interrupts the guard's report. I stare down at the fire extinguisher in my hands. It's one of those small ones that are kept in kitchens or small homes. My wide eyes hover on the guard crumpled on the ground before flickering up to the awe of Hannah's face. Scott stares from behind her shoulder, his expression priceless.

"We have to move." I manage to say as Hannah grabs hold of Kayla's raised arms and starts pushing her further down the hall. I can't stop staring at the guard on the ground, waiting for the rise and fall of his chest to make sure he's okay. I think I see it, the subtle movement, but it doesn't make me feel much better.

"Alexandra, come on," Hannah calls as boots echo in the adjacent hallway, getting louder and louder as they get closer and closer.

My feet finally wake up, and I take off down the hallway behind Hannah, Scott, and Kayla. Right. Then Left. Another Right. Hannah seems to know where we're going. I think we're running in circles.

We turn another corner, and Hannah runs directly into a body, the three of us halting behind her before causing a pileup. Another security guard, this one holding a baton.

"Run!" Hannah screams at us as she throws herself at the guard. As a distraction? An attack? I don't see what happens because Kayla screeches and takes off in the direction we just came from. She links her arm through mine as she moves, so I have no choice but to follow her.

"Kayla, we need to help Hannah!" I call after her, but I don't stop running, and neither does she.

# THIRTY-ONE

**I KEEL OVER, TRYING** to catch my breath. We've put distance between us and the guard, lost ourselves somewhere in the web of the Institute. But it's a false sense of safe.

"What are we going to do? What are we going to do?" Kayla paces frantically, her words jumbling together.

We seem to be back where we started, I recognize the administration section. But we're alone. Scott didn't follow us. Of course, he didn't. He wouldn't have abandoned Hannah like we did. Some friends we are.

My heart pounds, matching the pounding in my head. Kayla's moaning. It's an awful high-pitched whine.

"Kayla, be quiet. Someone will hear you."

As if on cue, there's a loud bang from the other side of the door I'm leaning against. I jolt away, my heart in my throat. I brace to run again, to dodge another guard's baton, but it's Logan's face framed in the window. His piercing, familiar eyes staring out at me.

My legs go weak, and the tension drains from my body until I realize his eyes are fluttering back and forth between Kayla and me. They are vacant and surprised, and they don't know me.

He doesn't recognize me.

Faint footsteps careen down another passage, then Kayla's voice, high and urgent. "Come on, Alexandra. We have to go."

"I'm not leaving here without him," I hiss. I try the handle of the door, but it's locked. I try Headmaster Johnson's pass, but the angry red light on the swipe box continues to stare at me, taunting me. I dig my nails around the edge to pry it open. I have no way to get in, but I need to find one and quick.

I slam my fist against the plastic cover, and there's a little crack. Logan's face takes up the whole window, trying to see what I'm doing, his eyes mirroring my desperation. Kayla is nervously pacing behind me again. I ball my hand into a fist and slam it into the lock pad again and again and again until that hairline crack becomes larger. Until a small piece of it breaks away, and I'm able to stick a finger underneath the outside plate and pop it off.

Kayla's peering over my shoulder at the mess of wires and metal endpoints. "Just grab some wires and pull," she huffs in my ear. I wish it were that easy.

"What if I pull the wrong one and he's stuck in there?" I rack my brain for any knowledge leftover from school. Did we ever learn about circuits or wires? Something to help make sense of how this works.

There's banging on the door again. Logan tries yelling something through the window, but it's nothing but a muffled noise. I mime my hand to my ear, showing I can't hear him.

He takes a big inhale and then blows his breath out onto the glass, the warmth causing condensation over the window, obstructing his face. Then ghostly letters appear:

## SHORT CIRCUIT

"He says to short the circuit." Kayla reads out loud, helpfully. "How do you short a circuit? What is a circuit?" She's twisting her hair around her fingers, her nervous tick. With all the running, her coiffed updo has fallen out, and small pieces frame her face. She blows one away and reaches back under her ponytail for a bobby pin to secure them back in place.

"Kayla! You genius—give me that." I grab for the bobby pin, bending it out of shape before she argues. All these wires would create a circuit. If I disrupt that, it should cut off the flow. "Stand back," I warn as I jam the bobby pin into the control box.

There's a massive spark and a potent and unfamiliar stench of melting electronics as the pad smokes. We take another step back as the pad sparks again, this time with a sudden buzz and then a metal clunk. The door screeches on its hinges as it's pushed open, and Logan comes flying out. He stumbles and I reach out to steady him.

"Logan!" I'm so relieved to see him I can't think to say anything else, can't think to move, despite Kayla's impatient pacing.

"Where am I?" He asks, but his words are cut off by a loud *boom* that radiates through the corridor. Kayla doesn't wait for us; she takes off running.

Sirens start to wail. The lights overhead flash from their dirty yellow to a jarring red. Up ahead, there's a twirling red light above a giant fire door.

A group of heavily booted feet comes barreling around the corner, catching us at a standstill. The security guards see us, and they are yelling.

"Go, go, go!" Kayla yells, not even pausing, as she heads towards the fire door. She crosses the threshold, Logan right behind her, her hand reaching back through the doorway to hover over a giant red button to activate the door.

"Hurry up!" She yells. And I run as fast as I can. I have plenty of time to reach them, but not enough time to dodge the figure that steps out of the doorway and right into my path.

I collide with it, my entire world spinning as my feet go out from under me. I land roughly on my side on the hard cement floor.

Logan yells. He's trying to come back for me, the kindness in him wanting to rescue a girl he doesn't even remember. But Kayla pulls him back through the fire door, her hand moving towards the big red button, looking at me, eyes big and wide.

"I'm sorry." She mouths as she hits the button, and the door swiftly closes.

A myriad of thoughts run through my head, so many images

and memories and last words I want to yell, but I say nothing.

A pair of red-soled heels step into my line of sight and then the distinct sound of a gun being cocked.

I'm curled in a fetal position on the floor, my hands covering my ears, my eyes clenched shut, waiting for the inevitable gunshot. But it doesn't come. Slowly, I ease open my eyes to the women standing over me.

"Miss Shaw," she says my name like she knows me. And of course, she does. She's known many versions of me.

"Dr. Anderson." I greet her with the same calmness she gave me.

She brushes off the guards and waits for me to climb to my feet. I move slowly. My body screams in warning, but so does my mind. This woman literally stood in the way of my escape, and now I'm standing alone with her.

She motions me towards the door she stepped out of, her name on a plaque towards the top. It's wide open and welcoming, though, in my current situation, it's nothing but foreboding. The only reason I even enter is because slumped over in one of the chairs is Hannah. Her blond hair a mess, dark smudges across her face. Wondering whether it's dirt or blood makes me nauseous. What the hell happened to her? Scott is with her, though he is in much better shape.

"Won't you please have a seat?" Dr. Anderson tries again, but I don't move. I can't move. I won't let myself get cornered in a smaller room. There will be no making it out at all if that happens.

"I'd rather stand here, thank you."

She seems to want to force the issue, but she lets it go and walks behind her desk, kicking off her heels before sitting down. It gives a false sense of safety like she won't chase us if we run, but there's no way there aren't guards waiting for us outside this door. "Not exactly the most appropriate footwear to counteract a terrorist attack, are they."

"Terrorist attack? Is that what you're going to pretend this is?" I almost can't believe it, though I don't know why I'm surprised. There's too much for them to lose if the truth gets out about these unconstitutional trials.

"All of these patients, they were all in a bad way before we met them. They were likely going to die. By their own hand, most of them. What we're doing here, it's going to change lives. It *is* changing lives." She is so earnest when she speaks, putting her full belief into their practice.

"Well, that clearly doesn't work." I point out.

"Well, it hasn't been exactly what we hoped, but no need to worry about that much longer." She pauses, shifting her focus to Hannah. "Headmaster Johnson said there was a rat in the school, some critter scurrying around, chewing on things they shouldn't. We never would have guessed it'd be you, though, little mouse."

Hannah stares at her defiantly but doesn't say a word, daring her to keep talking.

"I'm sure you think you're helping them, but how much did you help Kyle? That was you, right? You made him question the Academy, whether his aggression was really a part of him. You made him doubt everything, and that caused him to trigger. He would have jumped right off that cliff if they didn't reach him in time." Dr. Anderson seems to be gloating, and Hannah's body stiffens. I hadn't noticed it before, but her shoulders sag. She must have been carrying this guilt with her these last few days.

"There's no way you could have done this yourself. There's more of you, right? Tell you what. Since you've always been a quiet, good student, I'll cut you a deal. How about you give up your friends, and I won't have you reset again." She offers, a strange smile spreading across her face.

"Go for it. You have to know by now that doesn't work on me anymore." Hannah's acting smug, but her confidence is wavering.

"Yes, we are aware that our procedure hasn't been working to its full potential. But you don't have to worry about that anymore. We've fixed it. Our overwriting process is better than ever. No more slips. Permanent reformation. And it's been working quite well, as you probably could tell, Alexandra." Dr. Anderson has the audacity to smile at us.

Logan. She's talking about Logan. Permanent reformation.

Hannah's face loses all color. Her breaths become shallow, and she starts mumbling, a skipping record. "No, no, no, no."

I catch Scott out of the side of my eye. He's sitting there open-mouthed. "Do something," I growl at him, as if there's anything he can do. I'm not even sure he knows what is going on anymore.

I give him credit though, he stands up, but Dr. Anderson makes a small whistling noise and the guards in the hallway enter the room. They head towards Hannah and drag her out of the seat.

"No, stop! What are you doing? Where are you taking her?" I yell, but my voice is as useless as Hannah struggles against the guard's firm grip.

Her eyes find mine, glassy orbs desperately seeking help, but I can't do anything. I can't move. I can't reassure her. I know where they will take her, what they will do to her, but not what comes next. What will happen to the Academy, to the Institute? Is this it for the program, or will they permanently wipe our memories and start over? I stare after her, not losing track of her. I can tell, she's preparing for the worst. She's telling me goodbye.

Her lips move, just barely, but I see it, can hear her whisper, "Don't forget me. Please don't forget me." And then she's gone.

# THIRTY-TWO

**"NOW, WHAT DO WE** do with you two?" Dr. Anderson muses, towering over Scott and me. I'm stuck in my chair, eyes glued to the door Hannah was dragged through. A silly part of me keeps waiting for her to come back, any minute now. But I know she won't. I know she's gone. That my selfish need to rescue Logan has led Hannah to her end.

Well, the end of Hannah as we know her, if what Dr. Anderson says about this permanent procedure is true.

"You can let us go, no harm no foul," Scott says, which draws an eye roll from Dr. Anderson. I want to roll my eyes too. Where was this bravado when it came to Hannah's freedom? "It was just a suggestion." He skitters back into his shell, looking down at his hands, picking idly at his nails.

"If only it were that easy… with everyone else, their parents signed away their say. We make the choices that are best to their recovery. But you two, since your parents are actively involved in the process, we don't have that same freedom." She's pacing around the room like she's trying to make a life changing decision, but I get the feeling that the decision is already made for her.

"You have no choice but to let us go, do you? You have to send us back to our parents." I say, the truth coming clear for me. This should be an exciting revelation. Scott seems reassured by it, anyway, knowing that his father is likely not going to do anything too drastic to him.

But me. My mother. That's a whole other story. I have no idea what she'll want to do with me. She's already agreed to this procedure more than once. Agreed to putting fake memories in my head as well, about my dad. I don't have the same comfort in this solution as Scott does.

"You are the head of this program, but you don't have the control over it, do you?" I ask again, and Dr. Anderson doesn't correct me. "You don't have to do it, you know. You don't have to be a part of this if it's gone beyond what you are comfortable with. There's still a chance for you to let us go, to walk away, before it's too late."

Dr. Anderson frowns at me. For a minute, I think she might have sympathy for me. That maybe she won't send me back into the lion's den. But with a little shake of her head, she whistles again and two more guards step into the room.

"Take them back to the Academy. Let their parents deal with them as they wish."

The guards step forward, yanking us from our chairs. I try to fight, wriggle free, but the hands clamped around my bicep is too firm, I can't do anything but follow their lead.

We're taken to an unmarked white van and tossed into the back. There are two rows of bench seats, perfectly designed to transport a number of students to an Institute to be brainwashed, perhaps.

It's still dark out, we've been in the Institute for a good portion of the night. When the guard turns on the van, the clock tells me it's just past 5 am. I haven't been awake this early in… my entire life.

I wriggle in the seat to get into a more comfortable position. Scott is quiet beside me. His silence makes the absence of Hannah and Kayla louder. Guilt cuts into my chest, wrapping itself around my lungs. I can't breathe.

I should have known better than to think my plan would work, that I could get us all in and out of that place. I put my friends in danger, begged them to help me knowing they wouldn't say no. I'm so selfish and careless and a terrible friend.

And Logan didn't even remember me. Of all things, that is what I think about. The crushing realization that he was permanently reset, that I was wiped from his mind forever. I wonder if Logan and Kayla made it out safely. I let this tiny hope nourish me because, from the way things seem, it's the only hope I have left.

I run through the worst-case scenarios in my head. Will I be locked away in the basement and disappear into the stuff of legend, stories whispered between students as a warning? Maybe we will move to another town, start this entire process over again.

Either way, I see no positive outcome for me, no option that sees me going back to school on Monday. If there is even a school to go back to.

The school gates are closed as we pull up. I look out the window at the stone wall, the place that Kayla and Hannah wait for me every morning.

I think of Kayla's as she closed that door. It wasn't cruel, but it was isolating all the same. She saved herself. That's what people are wired to do, right? How can I be mad at her for that? And yet I am, because that door didn't just leave me behind. It cut off my future, the path that saw me get out of all of this in one piece. That saw me with Logan again.

The car pulls through the gates and up towards the back of the Academy. Tears burn at the edge of my eyes. The familiarity of defeat sinks into my shoulders, making them ache with a heaviness I haven't felt in years.

We're met by Headmaster Johnson and my mother. She's standing a little behind him, her posture stiff and reserved, a hint of that resentment in her eye I've come to know so well. They're standing in front of the red door that Logan and I crashed through when we made our initial escape from the school basement. It's propped open by something, the staircase behind it dark and looming.

The guards get out first. I wait for my door to be yanked open and large, glove-covered hands to reach in and grab me. Drag me out. The other guard grabs Scott from the back seat. Headmaster

Johnson seems pained to see Scott in this position, but my mother's expression is harder to read. I can't tell if she's surprised or if she even cares.

Headmaster Johnson steps forward. I think he's going to inspect his son, but he approaches me instead. "Alexandra, I'm sorry to see you here this morning. These... failures in the program, they are not something we are proud of here at the Academy."

"I'm not a failure," I spit out, wriggling my body a little. The guard holding me adjusts his grip slightly but firmly.

"Well, you're clearly not a success. This anger, this disobedience, none of this is what the program represents. We can't have you running around, triggering everyone's memories, resetting people's lives. There are protocols and rules for a reason, and you're jeopardizing everything we have all worked so hard for."

I snort. This is definitely not something to be proud of.

"You and your allies have successfully thrown an awfully expensive and frustrating wrench into our program. And in the process, caused a disturbance in the one place that could make it all better for you, make you forget any of this ever happened."

"I don't know what you're talking about. This has nothing to do with me," I offer, trying to stall.

"And yet you've led a group of vigilantes to break into a medical facility and risk seriously injuring many sick kids."

I almost laugh at him calling everyone there sick. No matter what happened in their past, it doesn't justify what they are doing to them now. "If anyone is sick, it's not those kids. Besides, that wasn't me." I volley back, but his expression doesn't change. He certainly doesn't believe me.

"Alexandra, two of my guards brought you here. Dr. Anderson has already called ahead. We clearly know you were at the Institute."

"Then why are you wasting my time talking about things you already know?" I spit, and Headmaster Johnson nearly throws his hands up in frustration. For a Headmaster of a school full of teenagers, he surely doesn't have much patience for dealing with one. He collects himself and turns to face me again.

"How about we show each other a little more respect and tell the truth?"

"Does that go for all of us? If I tell you the truth, will you tell me the truth? All of you?" Headmaster Johnson nods quickly, but it's my mother I'm watching. It's her eyes that get a little sharper, untrusting.

I keep focused on her as I confess. "Fine, you're right. I went to the Institute to rescue Logan. Because I know. I know everything. I know what you are doing to kids there, I know what you did to me."

Headmaster Johnson was expecting this and doesn't give me much of a reaction, but my mother's body reacts on instinct. I see it, briefly she struggles for composure, crumbling a little bit.

I think about what Logan told me, how she came unraveled after the accident, and wonder whether this is how it starts. If she is thinking about that, too. Realizing that her stoic composure is slipping. Her true self, her true emotions, clawing at the cracks, ripping her thick skin away in pieces, desperate to get out.

Everyone is quiet for a moment, and the energy in the air shifts. My heart is racing, and yet, I'm steady. Every moment of the last few weeks has been leading up to this. Every moment of my life has been leading up to this.

There's something inside of me now, something powerful, something strong. It's pushing me to finally pull myself away from the life that I wrapped safely around me. One that belittled me and kept me small. But one that I knew. That was always consistent. That I felt a sick sort of comfort in.

"I told you what you wanted to know. Now it's your turn." Headmaster Johnson is about to say something, but I cut him a look that shuts him right up. Instead, he takes a small step away. He crosses over to Scott and puts his hand on his son's shoulder, a little comfort. The kind of comfort I've never gotten from either of my parents.

My eyes are level on my mother. She shifts uncomfortably, waiting for my words.

"Tell me the truth, mother. For once in your life, tell me the truth about everything that's happened."

"Everything that has... I don't know what you mean?" she says, but I know she does. She is still trying to tease out exactly what *I* know. Hoping that she can still keep her distance from this, pretend that she has nothing to do with this.

"I know what really happened with the accident. That you were the one driving. About why you sent me to that Institute."

My mother's knees give out a little and seeing it makes me stand a little taller. The more she shrinks in front of me, the bigger I can grow.

"Alexandra, I sent you there because I didn't want to lose you. You were going to die."

"No, I didn't need to be sent to a secret experimental facility to recover from a car accident. You sent me there because if I survived, you didn't want to lose me to the rest of the world that was out there waiting for me. You wanted to control me like you couldn't control my father. You were too scared to be left alone. Please, tell me the truth."

She swallows a sob. Part of me is overcome with relief, a small victory talking openly about all of this, about the Institute, about my mother's actions. I never would have had the courage to stand up to her before, to take back some control. But it's easy to do when you have nothing left.

She inhales deeply and holds it for a long time. I don't think she will answer; I don't think she will fold in on herself and speak honestly. But she does; she opens her mouth, and she looks at me a little sadly as she speaks.

# THIRTY-THREE

**"YOU HAVE TO IMAGINE** what my life was like, back then," my mother starts, her voice a false sense of even. "You may find this hard to believe, but I was wildly carefree, once. A young girl from the wrong side of town, on the brink of womanhood who no one knew what to do with. And your father, well he came from the right side of town. His family was wealthy, and he was given everything he could ever want."

She's never talked so openly about my dad before. I never knew he was from a wealthy family. A small, selfish part of me bristles at this information. Our life could have been so different back then if we had his family's money. I might have been able to get away from her earlier, spared myself all this pain and trauma.

"Of course, he wanted what he couldn't have. Tempted by the unknown, a creature so unlike any of his friends and especially his family. I wanted nothing to do with him, which only made him want me more. Do you know what that feels like? To be so desired by someone? It's intoxicating. So intoxicating, that eventually, I was swept up in the promise of a better life than the life that was keeping me small. The life a woman like me deserved.

"We married quickly, much to his parent's dismay. He knew this would mean we would live without their support, without their wealth. We were convinced that love was enough, because we were madly in love. The kind of obsessive love that feels infinite. The kind of love that is so blinding that you don't see that there is nothing else left if it begins to simmer out." Her voice cracks at this and she takes a breath to steady her nerves. I have a hard time picturing my mother this in love with someone. She's never seemed affectionate at all. Always so guarded and protective of herself. A switch flips and suddenly, I can see right through her thick skin to the real woman she was, all along. A woman in love, who somehow ended up with a broken heart.

"When we got married, he wanted so much from me. All of my attention, all of my love. I did everything I could to make him happy. Everything I thought I had to, even if it meant forgetting about myself. But it was never enough. And then there was a baby. You. This was supposed to make everything better, make us a real family. But a baby is loud and needy and always around. Always pulling my attention away. I was exhausted, weighed down by responsibility and no sleep. I cringed at his touch and turned away from him. The effervescent woman he fell in love with, who he gave everything up for, was gone."

A darkness settles in her words as she remembers me as a

baby. How I needed her. Someone else, taking things from her she didn't want to give.

"The resentment was heavy, he blamed me for how his life turned out, for the choices we made together. It was hard not to daydream about how different it would be for him, he said. If his family name still offered the family comfort, a bigger house, a better life. Even if it meant I wasn't in it. Those daydreams quickly turned into plans, which quickly turned into reality. One morning he left a letter on the kitchen table as he left for work. Left the house, left his family and all his belongings. He never came back."

"And you were left with me," I say flatly. "The child you never wanted, but felt you had to have, to please a man who betrayed you."

"I gave up my life for you, you see that don't you? I could have made other choices. I could have left him first. I thought about it. I could have left for the city like most of my friends did. I could have spent my days painting; did you know I used to paint? I could have spent my nights in the arms of different men. But I chose you. You ruined my life, and I still chose you. And I will not let anyone ruin you like he ruined me. I've sacrificed everything to protect you." With this, my mother puts her hands on her waist. Defiant. That's that.

My blood boils.

"But look what you've done to me, look where we are! You aren't protecting me; you are imprisoning me!" Tears start to swell again, building in my throat.

Her arms jerk forward, like she wants to reach out to me. To brush the hair from my face, take me into her arms. Motherly actions that have never been a part of her repertoire. But she quickly retracts them, wrapping them around herself instead.

"I never meant to hurt you. I just couldn't lose you." It's a whisper, nearly lost on the wind. But I hear her words, and in them, her truth. She thought she was protecting me. Didn't know what else to do to make it so I didn't leave her, like my father did.

"So then, for once in your life, stop lying and tell me the truth."

"What do you want to know, Alexandra? What is even left? You're right, okay? I couldn't stand the thought of you leaving me behind. I am nothing without you. I have nothing! Do you know what that does to a person? Someone who has dedicated their entire life to someone else? It tears them in two. It rips their heart into pieces. I didn't think I could go through that again. The Institute offered me an opportunity, and I took it."

At the mention of the Institute, Headmaster Johnson's head jerks. He and Scott have been standing off to the side, looking everywhere but at us. Ignoring the two women in the middle of the school yard nearly screaming at each other. But I don't care if I'm making a scene, I don't care if we're airing all our dirty laundry. This is a conversation we need to have. One we've needed to have for years now.

"Dedicated? You have done nothing but manipulate me my entire life! Playing mind games and messing with my head. And when that wasn't enough, you literally had people cut into my head and alter my memories! You made me think I killed my father!"

"I needed to make you weak, I needed to make you dependent, I needed to make you love me. How else was I going to make you love me? I am not lovable!" She's pulling at the hem of her sweater to keep from reaching out to me. To keep herself in one piece, the cracks threatening to make her crumble completely.

I want to tell her I do love her, that I always have, but I don't know if it's the truth. I don't know what is real anymore and what are ideas other people have implanted in me.

It seems unimaginable that after everything that has happened, everything I've been through, that there is a little bit of me that could love her. I'm seeing her at her weakest. Her insecurities and trauma and her own self-hatred spilling out over her. It's hard to turn away, to hate her entirely.

I try to think about what our life could have been. What our relationship could have been, if instead of avoiding each other, we had allowed ourselves to lean on each other. To work through things together. But I was too young when he left the first time, too jaded when he kept leaving. The seeds of betrayal and malice had already been planted.

We never had a chance.

"You need to let me go, mother. Please, let me go," I beg, barely a whisper.

The wind has picked up, my hair whipping around my face. I'm chilled to the bone, but I can't tell if it's the temperature or the emotional weight being lifted that is leaving me feeling weak and frail.

My mother is still, her eyes more alive than I've ever seen

them. She's looking at me with love and affection through a watery pane. And I think she might concede. She might let me go.

But then I see that mask slip back over her face. Her expression goes dead, and she picks herself back up. She turns back to the headmaster, putting her hand on his arm gently. "Rick, maybe we should take this inside. This is getting out of control."

He hesitates slightly, but then nods.

I can't go into that basement. I know this. If they put me in one of those rooms, I'm never getting out of there. I'll never find Logan.

I'll never get my life back.

Headmaster Johnson turns to the red door, shuffling Scott downstairs in front of him. My mother stands there, watching me as the guard closes in on me, grabbing my upper biceps again preparing to drag me forward.

But before he can take a step, I quickly raise both my arms up over my head. I bring them down with all the strength, so my elbows cut back and stab him right in the abdomen. He grunts loudly and loosens his grip. He doesn't let go, but I push off him hard enough to break away. I start running as fast as I can across the grass towards the forest.

The guard recovers quickly, and now both are right behind me, cutting further to my right to head off my path. I shift my direction and head back towards the other end of the peninsula. But Headmaster Johnson and my mother have started running up that side to cut my escape off on that end.

I stop dead in the middle, a few paces away from each of

them. They all stop running as well, leaving me cornered, my back against the cliffs, my escape thwarted.

Spray from the rough waters below kiss my cheeks, but I quickly realize that it's tears. I'm crying. I'm breathless. My legs are aching and begging me to surrender, but I can't surrender. I can't give up my future, my freedom, and stay here with her.

I keep looking around frantically at the guards, my mother, the headmaster. Scott has disappeared, ran for his life hopefully, but that leaves me with no one on my side. No clear way out of this. Everyone has started inching slowly towards me, their hands up in a calming motion, trying not to scare me. I'm trapped and cornered, frantic and desperate for escape.

It's the same way I felt that night, trapped in the car with them. I remember this same hopelessness, the need for an escape. And then I see that night again, remember what really happened.

She was driving. I couldn't breathe. The air inside the car was muggy and suffocating. They were fighting. I was gulping back tears, trying to find some fresh air to ease the burning in my throat. All of that is true. But the real scene comes rushing back to me.

*We're in the car—the three of us. Rain threatening to fall, the sky a purplish black. They're arguing. It's all they do lately. About him leaving, again.*

*"Leave me alone!" I yell, clasping my hands over my ears, burying my head in my lap.*

*My entire life was slipping away from me. My entire future, a mirror of my past. Nothing would change. He will keep leaving, she will keep blaming me, continue to control me, manipulate me, never let me go.*

*"I won't let you leave me." A whisper, falling from my mother's lips. The even, dangerous tone is enough to make me look up.*

*Her hands gripped the steering wheel, a fury so hot her knuckles were white. I couldn't rip my eyes away, which is how I saw it. That momentary jerk, the wheel turning slightly to the right. Enough to make it seem like an accident, but very clearly not.*

*There was no time to react; the car went barreling into the forest. But instead of thinking of what I could do, what might help, I thought about how I would never get away from her now.*

I'm numb. Frozen. The scene on repeat in my mind. She caused the accident. Not the rain. She killed my father, so he wouldn't leave. She could have killed me, too.

There's a strange sense of calm that comes over me with this realization.

I think about all the students who have gone wild, who have found their way to this very place. I wonder whether they felt this same sense of peace as the wind whipped through their hair. The water drumming against the rocks below. Their past laid out entirely before them.

I think about Hannah, hoping the network she helped build

can swoop in and save her from being erased forever. Of Kayla, hoping that when she ran, she never stopped running until she hit the city, somewhere further, somewhere to start new.

But most of all I think of Logan. I remember the time we had together, the real memories that got me through all of this. Memories that comforted me and reminded me of who I am, who I really am, and that I'm worth it. I wish that I could see him again, but I'll cling to the fact that he got out. That I saved him. And now he can rebuild. Become anything he wants, anything that he chooses.

As they continue to move in on me, I match their steps with small ones of my own. My calves press up against the stone wall now, the only thing between me and the cliff's edge.

I climb up onto the wall. Horror possesses my mother's face as she realizes what is about to happen, and she runs. Her mouth is forming large O shapes, but I can't hear anything against the wind. She raises her arms out frantically in front of her, reaching for me, but she's too far.

I raise my own arms, but not to her. I raise them above me as I lean back. The momentum carries me up and over the edge of the cliff like a graceful dive off a stage into the sea of awaiting hands at a crowded concert.

And I'm free.

# Author's Note

Dear Reader,

Thank you for reading my book! I am an indie author, which means that I'm not affiliated with any traditional publishing house. This book was written, produced, published, and promoted at my own expense.

If you enjoyed this book, I humbly ask you to consider helping me reach more readers. Ratings and reviews on Amazon, Goodreads and other book platforms are a tremendous support. as is posting on social media or requesting the book from your local library or independent bookstore.

You can also sign up for my newsletter for information on new releases, giveaways, special offers and bonus content: www.alloydspanton.ca

Thank you so much for your support!

# Acknowledgements

This book isn't autobiographical, but I borrowed so many things from my life for it, wrote inside jokes and stole people's names. I wanted to surround myself with everything that means the most to me, the things and people that comfort me. So, I have a lot of people to thank.

Amy (Feral Girl Books), you are the coolest. Your writing and industry knowledge is unparalleled, and I feel so lucky to have you in my corner. It was an absolute joy going feral with you.

Emma Jane (EJL Editing), who rounded up my misused grammar and showed it (and me) who's boss. You brought this all together and were so awesome to work with. (Look, I didn't use 'like' once!)

Jenn, Marina and the Qamber Designs team, for not only understanding my cover vision, but bringing it to life in an unforgettable way.

Livy, I'm forever grateful that you found me flailing out in the Twitterverse and reeled me into the most chaotic, clever, accepting and wildly supportive writing group. Joining WTS was the best thing I ever did, and I love you all: Affy, Alexandra, Amanda, Brekke, Bri, Carly, Des, Kandra, Kristina, Morgan, Nic, and Sarah June.

Taylor, my publishing Yoda. I would still be trying to figure out margins and page numbers if it weren't for you.

Sarah E-P., one of the most positive people I've ever met. It means so much to have you shine a little bit of your light on me and my words.

Rach, you were one of the first people I ever shared my words with. Thank you for being you – compassionate, supportive, and really bloody witty.

Em, merci de me connaître et de m'amener au plus profond des niveaux. Te rencontrer a été une belle chose et tu es une belle personne.

Alaina, my writing bestie, meeting you was life changing. Without you on this journey, well, there'd be no journey. Thank you for challenging me, pushing me, taming my storms, and always understanding me and my vision. I couldn't have done any of this without you, seriously.

E. Whelly, your support, encouragement and advice has been so invaluable, I'm so lucky to have met you.

Rachelle and Ceinwen, your content and books have been such an inspiration to me and gave me the courage to put myself out there. Please keep doing what you do.

Jake, I owe so much of my adult life to you inviting me to join that ball team and helping me find my footing in this scary city.

Scott, thanks for letting me use your name, even though I didn't ask you. I'm still mad about that Radiohead concert, though.

Omar, your support and friendship mean the world to me. I can't wait for you to direct this movie.

Terri, your friendship and support is everything. If in 10 years I'm half the person you are, I will consider myself lucky.

Veronica, for reading all the books with me. Jen, for introducing me to something called Twilight. And Aila, for watching all the adaptations to keep the conversations alive. The years with you all have been wine filled and ridiculous and one day I will write a book about them.

Dave, thank you for putting up with my rants and for always giving me a safe, non-judgmental space to fall apart in. Your taste in music may suck, but I genuinely would be so lost without your friendship.

Nov, my sister-wife. The grounding force that brings me back to myself. Words can't express how much you mean to me. Thank you for sharing your cabin in the woods for my writing retreats. And Michael, for putting up with me.

Glenn, my brother, and trusted confidante. You were one of my very first readers and very first believers. You talked me down from some ledges and pushed me to keep going when I wanted to give up – in life and in writing.

My parents, Kathy and Ron, who have endlessly loved and supported me with everything I've done. Who spent endless hours cheering for me at the ball diamond and piano recitals and the swimming pool and the curling rink and the skating rink and the bowling alley and the gymnastic club. Who took me to Disneyland and the Caribbean and road trips across Canada. I really wish I could remember it all. I love you.

And finally, my partner Jeremy. The one I could never forget. Who keeps me full of love and laughter, so I don't lose myself completely when writing about dark things. **I love you most**.

# About the Author

Ash Lloyd Spanton lives in Toronto, Canada with her partner, a growing library, and their cat.

She currently writes for the broadcast industry—behind the scenes, not the cool content stuff. Her books are generally dark and broody, and usually about angry women.

The Unforgettable Alexandra Shaw is her debut novel.

Follow her on Instagram, Twitter and TikTok at @alloydspanton or visit www.alloydspanton.ca for more information.